Mermaid Park

Mermaid Park

BETH MAYALL

razOr
bill

Mermaid Park

RAZORBILL

Published by the Penguin Group
Penguin Young Readers Group
345 Hudson Street, New York, New York 10014, U.S.A.
Penguin Group (USA) Inc., 375 Hudson Street, New York, New York 10014, U.S.A.
Penguin Books Canada Ltd, 10 Alcorn Avenue, Toronto, Ontario,
Canada M4V 3B2 (a division of Pearson Penguin Canada, Inc.)
Penguin Books Ltd, 80 Strand, London WC2R 0RL, England
Penguin Ireland, 25 St Stephen's Green, Dublin 2, Ireland
(a division of Penguin Books Ltd)
Penguin Group (Australia), 250 Camberwell Road, Camberwell,
Victoria 3124, Australia (a division of Pearson Australia Group Pty Ltd)
Penguin Books India Pvt Ltd, 11 Community Centre, Panchsheel Park,
New Delhi – 110 017, India
Penguin Group (NZ), Cnr Airborne and Rosedale Roads, Albany,
Auckland 1310, New Zealand (a division of Pearson New Zealand Ltd)
Penguin Books (South Africa) (Pty) Ltd, 24 Sturdee Avenue, Rosebank,
Johannesburg 2196, South Africa

Penguin Books Ltd, Registered Offices: 80 Strand, London WC2R 0RL, England

10 9 8 7 6 5 4 3 2 1

Interior design by Christopher Grassi

Library of Congress Cataloging-in-Publication Data
Mayall, Beth.
Mermaid Park / by Beth Mayall.
    p. cm.
Summary: Sixteen-year-old Amy escapes family difficulties by immersing herself in
her job at a mermaid-themed water show.
ISBN 1-59514-029-8 (hardcover)
[1. Swimming—Fiction. 2. Summer employment—Fiction. 3. Family problems—Fiction.
4. Wildwood (N.J.)—Fiction.] I. Title.
PZ7.M45725Me 2005
[Fic]—dc22

                                                                    2004026077

Printed in the United States of America

For Drew

CHAPTER

PACKED IN THE BACK OF OUR FAMILY FREAK-SHOW WAGON O' FUN, I was coming to terms with the fact that I was not a nice person. A nice person wouldn't have just spent two hours wishing severe, incurable illness upon Rebecca Shoemaker, the friend who'd bailed on spending three days with me on this family trip to the Jersey shore.

It's not like she would've had a good time anyway. For one, we were only forty-five minutes into the drive to Wildwood, and already my stepdad Tom's traffic fixation had blossomed into full-fledged paranoia.

"What's this?" Mom had asked from the front seat early on in the trip, holding up a map covered in fluorescent yellow highlights between two long red fingernails.

"What's it look like?" Tom said, grabbing it and swinging it in front of her face before wedging it into the stack of receipts and paper bags on the dashboard.

Mom let out a tired sigh, and she shifted her weight to lean against the window. "We aren't just taking the Parkway?"

"The Parkway is for idiots. I found a back way."

"A back way, the entire way?" Mom mumbled into the window. We were already on a two-lane rural road through Chester County; woods stretched for miles on either side, and the speed limit was a mellow thirty-five. "Babe," she said, "Wildwood is over a hundred miles from here."

I shot a glance at my younger sister, Melissa, next to me, her sticky-sweaty thigh already unpleasantly stuck to mine. Her best friend, Trina, squeezed on the other side of Mel, was openly broiling in the brutal sunlight streaming through the passenger-side window. Their eyes went wide with panic, so I just glanced out the window, acting like it was no big deal. There was only so low I could sink—it was bad enough that Mel had convinced a friend to come along and I couldn't.

That morning Rebecca had called: "Don't hate me"—sounding fatigued and beaten by this round of asthma/mumps/strep/whatever—"but I think I'm dying."

Alarmist words indeed. Words that would've worried me coming from anyone but Rebecca, whose stay-at-home mom relished her daughter's sick days. On days Reb was home sick, I'd detour three blocks after school to drop off the homework assignments she'd missed. Last time, I'd knocked and waited on the front step, studying my handwriting on a loose-leaf sheet:

Math: Page 122, #s 1–29, odds only.

English: She says you can take a make-up vocab quiz on
Friday. BTW, I think I heard her call us the "sophomoric"

*class instead of the sophomore class—hello, Freudian
slip—but I was the only one who laughed, so I could be
hearing things.*

*Bio: Nada. Doc says to tell you to feel better soon. (Seriously,
that room stinks like formaldehyde—I don't know how you
stand it.)*

When there was no answer, I just went in, like always, and
was about to yell hello in the living room when I caught a glimpse
of Reb, sacked out on the couch, and her mom standing nearby,
contentedly eyeing her daughter's pale paper-thin skin, where you
could just about see the germ-carrying veins pumping toxins even
deeper into her 102-pound body. Her mom looked *happy*. It
creeped me out. Sometimes I thought she kept Reb in a bubble
on purpose, with too much hovering-mom TLC and too many
sunny afternoons spent inside watching *One Life to Live*.

In hour two of the drive, Mel started fidgeting her I-have-to-
pee dance. "Um," she said. She leaned up to the front seat and
put her elbows over the top. "How's it going up here?"

Mom reached up sleepily and touched the side of Mel's face.
"Good, sweetie. We'll be there soon."

Mel stayed there. I could see her watching Tom from the corner of her eye, trying to read his mood. His head was leaned back
on the headrest, relaxed. His favorite oldies rock station was on
the radio, and Mel said, "I like this song."

Tom nodded. It was a classic—the Rolling Stones, "I can't get
no sa-tis-fac-tion. . . ." Everybody knew this song.

Mel cocked her head to look at Tom and said, "I forget—who sings this again?"

I knew for a fact Mel had this same exact song on one of her workout tapes, which she'd categorized with the precision of an Ivy League librarian.

Mom turned to Tom, the same tilt to her head. She offered, "Is this the Who?"

Tom let out a laugh. "The Who? Are you serious?" He glanced at both of them, back and forth, waiting for a punch line.

Mom shrugged. Mel shrugged.

"This is classic Stones. Peak Mick Jagger." He pushed his wet lips out in an exaggerated pout. "I can't get no—whoa, sa! Tis! Fac! Shun!"

Mel collapsed into laughs, dropping her head over the front seat, resting on Tom's shoulder, blond hair streaming down, showing the sweaty part at the back of her neck. Laughing so hard, she couldn't even make a sound.

Tom shook his head, playing shame. "What am I going to do with you girls?"

Mom and Mel burst into laughter again.

A gas station appeared at the crest of the hill, and I saw Mel's head lift like she'd heard it coming. She simply pointed to it and said a soft, hopeful, "Ooh."

Mom picked up on it. "Let's make a quick stop."

Tom paused a beat and said, "Name another Stones song and I'll stop."

"Um." Mel looked at Mom.

"'We Will Rock You'?" Mom tried.

Tom made a loud game-show buzzer sound. "Thank you for playing!" He gunned the gas to speed up.

Mel strained, her brows pulled down. "I *know* I know one!"

I watched her too—she knew a dozen of them. I knew she was timing this whole thing.

"Ticktock ticktock," Tom said.

Mel's voice was low, with a question mark at the end— "'Brown Sugar'?"

Just in time, Tom slammed on the brakes and made a screeching right turn into the Getty station. Too loose-limbed from sleep, Trina slid across the sweaty vinyl seat and rammed right into my side. Gravel crunched and dust swarmed before we came to a stop.

Mel grabbed Trina and they darted for the side of the building, walking softly in bare feet over the gravel. Tom went inside for a Lotto ticket. The sudden stop had spread out all the crap in my messenger bag, and I lay down to see what I'd lost under the seat.

Suddenly I heard my mother scooting across to the driver's-side seat. "Hi, Officer," she said.

I froze in my hunched-down position as a gruff, male voice responded from just outside the rolled-down window, "That was dangerous, turning in here like that."

My mom did a delicate intake of breath. "I am so sorry about that," she said sincerely.

"You were speeding."

"My daughter and her friend had an emergency—do you have any children? They always want to stop every five minutes. Especially girls." Her voice had taken on a low, intimate tone, the one that made people feel like they were talking to someone they'd known forever. I stayed down, staring under the seat.

"You're lucky no one was standing here."

"Oh God—you're right," Mom agreed. "Thank God no one was here. Thank God no one was hurt." She was starting to sound upset.

The officer paused, and that's when I knew he'd fallen under the famous Mom spell. The one that got her coupons for free oil changes and complimentary Bloomin' Onions at Outback Steakhouse. I would squirm as the manager himself delivered the food to our table and stood there being thanked too many times.

"Well," he said.

"I am so grateful," Mom said. He might've been thinking, *Grateful for what?* But that didn't matter. The "grateful" always came before the big "thank you."

"You'll be more careful." This was a statement, not a question.

"I will," she said, her voice thickened, touched. "I truly can't thank you enough."

I heard the officer exhale self-consciously, a "shoo" sound. "Well," he said again. He cleared his throat. "Have a nice day, ma'am."

She slid into the passenger seat and I sat back up, watching as she flipped the visor down to check her reflection. A flush had come to her cheeks. Otherwise, I could see what the officer had seen—smooth skin barely marked by age, a small, delicate face where her eyes, a light gray-green, made you feel like you could see what she was thinking. Long blond hair with messy layers from the wind gave her a wildness I rarely saw. She caught me watching her in the mirror and winked at me.

"Another one bites the dust," I said under my breath, watching the cop get back in his mud-spattered cruiser.

Mom flipped up the visor and sang a little of that song "Another One Bites the Dust." "No, that's not the Rolling Stones," she said. "That's Queen, 1980."

I looked at her hard. Suddenly she had become a classic-rock guru?

"Was he going to give Tom a ticket?" I asked.

"I don't know. Maybe," she said.

"He should've," I mumbled. That was me, always mumbling.

"Amy," she said, turning her profile to me. "That's not nice."

I breathed. She was right. I had promised myself I was going to try to get along with everyone on this trip—including Tom. That part would be tough. Getting along with Mom would be a little easier. I could drop the mumbling. I could make nice with her. I ran through the list of topics in my head—no, asking about work always got her so serious. And Mom and I always argued when we talked about Mel. I played with the buckle on the strap of my bag, thinking. Suddenly, something came to me.

"So, you must be excited to go back to Wildwood, right?" My

mother had grown up spending her summers at the Jersey shore town, but this was her first time back in forever. "I still think it's weird you've never been to Lynne's motel before."

"She only got it a few years ago," Mom said.

"Yeah, I guess. But it's not like we couldn't have gone down to see Lynne there before she had the motel."

Lynne was my mom's godmother, even though she was actually only ten years older than my mother. It was a fun story—my mom's parents and Lynne's had been really good friends, and they always stayed together at the Jersey shore over the summers. When my mom was born, Lynne was ten years old, and she thought my mom was her little doll. So my grandparents asked Lynne to be my mom's godmother.

We'd seen Lynne pretty regularly when I was little, until my parents got divorced ten years ago. Then Mom started working full-time and dating—someone from work, then someone she met on the train, or once, a fireman who'd come to our house when we couldn't get the smoke detector to shut off after burning frozen pizza. On Mother's Day, though, Mom always cooked Lynne a big brunch that kept her busy at the stove for most of the morning. But we never went to see Lynne at Wildwood, where she lived year-round—Lynne always came to us.

Mom sat up straighter in her seat and turned to face me, the faintest sheen of perspiration on her cheeks. I cranked my window open to give her more air, and she smiled. "Once I married your dad, we just didn't travel. He didn't like the beach, and we had you guys, which was kind of a handful." A shadow passed over her eyes quickly—I knew she'd been the one in charge of taking care of us. Even now, the few times a year we visited Dad up in northern New Jersey, outside of New York City, he seemed unsure of how to handle us, always wearing the troubled expression of someone waiting in a long line. "Besides, I was tired of it. I used to go there every summer. After a while, you just get sick of the same thing all the time."

Over the front seat, I could see Mel coming back to the car. She and Trina had Blow Pops in their mouths, and Tom followed closely behind them.

Through the window, Mel said, "Got something for you." She tossed me a travel pack of Tampax. She did this on every vacation since the one time two years ago, on our first "family trip" to Atlantic City right after Tom and Mom got married. I had gotten my period in the car. I'd whispered this to Mom, who'd whispered to Tom, who'd handed me a stack of McDonald's napkins from the glove compartment. Mel had laughed so hard, I thought she might pee herself—probably partly from relief, because it could've just as easily been her, since we'd gotten our periods within one month of each other. Tom had kept looking in the rearview mirror, smiling at her, enjoying his joke. Mom had just shrugged to me, her lower lip pouting out to say "sorry."

What was I supposed to do? I'd crossed my legs and clenched my butt for the rest of the ride, my palms sweating through the stack of napkins I'd kept clenched in my fist, just in case. But it turned out I didn't need them. My anger, my hatred, my fear of bleeding through my shorts and all over the seat had shut my period down right at that moment. And while I knew magazines always said your period would be irregular for the first year, when mine didn't come back for three months, I blamed Tom. He had scared my period into remission.

Even now, my period was still pretty erratic. At least I knew there was no way I was pregnant, unless sperm could magically travel through a messy French kiss with Rob D'Ambrosio, even one that had left me badly in need of a rain slicker.

As always, I tossed the Tampax back to Mel. In her other hand was a postcard.

"Is that for Jason?" Mom asked.

"Yup," Mel said. She tucked the card into her slim leather purse. Jason was a kid in Mel's class who had cancer. She was always bringing stuff in for him to keep up his spirits.

"Amy, don't you think you should get one for Rebecca?" Mom said, with a sharp tone to her voice.

"Oh," I said. That was a good idea—she would think that was cool, a postcard from some random hick town in New Jersey. I reached for the door handle.

Just then, Tom slid into the front seat and announced, "The train is leaving." He started the engine. "Next stop, Wildwood."

I settled back down, pressing as close to the window—and as far from Mel—as possible. This past Mother's Day on Lynne's annual visit, Tom had come up with the idea for this trip. We were sitting around the kitchen table, the smell of bacon thick and unmoving in the air.

"So when are you going to roll out the welcome mat?" he'd asked Lynne around a mouthful of cheddar cheese omelet.

Lynne, sitting way across at the other end of the table, just continued to stir her black coffee, leveling him with a hard stare from her deep-set eyes. Her solid frame, draped in clothes the color of sunset reds and earthy browns, was comforting to have nearby. Sitting next to her, I heard her breath whistle in and out of her nose.

"You know," he continued, pressing it because that's what Tom did, he pushed until he won or something broke, "just a little vacation hospitality."

Mom didn't turn from the stove. In a tentative voice she said, "Babe, those rooms go for a hundred and fifty a night. It's peak season for Lynne." She had been dancing around money talk lately since Tom had gotten fired from his job cooking at a hotel in Center City.

"So we all cram into one room," Tom said quickly. "And maybe get a family discount since we're in good with the owner."

I cringed. Melissa played with the bacon on her plate, and I thought about getting up to open a window because the air was so thick. Mom said from the stove, "Anyway, you like Atlantic City, babe. The casinos, more space on the beach." I looked up at Mel to see if she was planning on jumping in to smooth this out. But no, her eyes were on Mom's tightly squared shoulders as she used a spatula to scramble our eggs roughly. "Wildwood is more for kids," Mom said.

Tom sat up and reached a hand to my face and one to Mel's. Finger pointing at each of us, up close. Lynne's eyes quickly lowered, and I hunched my shoulders to disappear. "And what are these?" he said. An exaggerated up-close inspection of Melissa's face, her blue eyes now downcast too. He picked up a strand of Mel's long straight hair and peered into her ear, his thick eyebrows lifted, wet lips in an O shape of mock surprise. "Are they—kids?"

Mom's lips pressed into a tight white line as she slid a heap of too-wet eggs onto my plate. A light yellow puddle of half-cooked liquid formed around them. My stomach made a strange shift, warning me what would happen if this came down my throat.

I wished she would tell him to shut up or take that frying pan and smack him on his broad forehead, which flushed pink when he was angry or excited, like right now. But she didn't. So I pushed my chair back with a satisfying screech and snapped, "I'm done."

"Where are *you* going?" Mom said sharply.

"Hm, I wonder," I said, my back to her, hoping she could hear the disgust in my voice that she let him talk to her like that. "Could be time for crayons. Could be Barbies. Could be writing to freaking Santa Claus to come and take me away from it all." As I pounded up the steps, the only other sound was the tinkling of Lynne's spoon still stirring in her cup.

The slamming sound of my door was never as loud and wall-cracking as I wanted it to be. My stomach was still knotted, so maybe it wasn't the eggs. I sat on the floor against my bed and braced my feet on either side of the mirror on the back of the door in case anyone tried to barge in after me. I hated how I looked when I got upset, and there it was looking right back at me in the mirror—angry red splotches blossoming on my chest and neck, my face redder than it should be, a human thermometer about to blow. On top, my mess of dark brown curls, way too long and overdue for a cut or a weed-whacking if you asked Mel.

It wasn't Tom's "kid" comment I cared about. I was sixteen but often mistaken for seventeen or eighteen. In my reflection I could see I had the soft-boned boredom of older girls, my shoulders shrugged high, head to one side, as if I was half asleep. It was a look I practiced. Cute and sleepy-eyed on some girls, it was a little lazy and angry on my thicker frame—but still pretty somehow. So I didn't care about him calling us kids. I just hated seeing Mom shrink from him like that.

Downstairs I heard the front door close, and I jumped up to peek out the blinds. Tom held the door of the station wagon open for Mel, bowing like her servant. Laughing, she slid into the front seat. They were probably going to Dairy Queen to get Blizzards, Mel's favorite, since I had ruined breakfast. She had smoothed over my scene and turned the situation to her favor. As usual. It was why I'd started mistrusting her. They'd bring back ice cream for Mom, too, probably, but not me.

So that's why Lynne had given us a free place to stay for three days. Although at the rate Tom's shortcut was going, we would miss most of day one.

His route was a *Family Circle* cartoon—a chunky dotted line lazily looping through neighborhoods, hopping fences, detouring through a doghouse. Once, passing a condemned apartment building, we caught a glimpse of the Garden State Parkway, an ocean of Fords and Buicks and Chevrolets, traffic at a standstill. Tom's chin lifted, and he laid on the horn for long, steady bleats—his arm waved wildly out the window. Or I assumed it was a wave and not his patented middle-finger salute.

Tom yelled, "Couldn't pay me enough to sit in that crap."

My mother, cooled by the four dashboard fans tilted her way, nodded gently in agreement or maybe to the music—who really knew?

Actually, I was working on a theory. I figured, how much worse could driving like normal people be? At least sitting in traffic together, clutching a handful of sweaty quarters and dimes for the toll—that would all *be* part of the vacation. Making eye contact with the strangers in the car next door, shrugging at each other like, *Traffic sucks. What can you do?*

But not Tom. That was not his way, so it wasn't ours either.

And if that meant our vacation would be spent chugging at thirty miles per hour behind a produce truck with exhaust plumes thick as melted tar, that's how it would be.

Even if it meant the three of us in the backseat would boil down to three little pools of sweat, scented of vanilla-melon lip gloss and Bain de Soleil.

CHAPTER Two

A TIRED, WHITEWASHED TWO-LANE BRIDGE WAS OUR GATEWAY TO Wildwood, stretching across marshland and pocked by flaking paint. Each plank bowed as it carried then released the weight of a car tire, and the rhythmic thunka-thunka-thunka sounded like a horse's gallop, more urgent than the drive really was.

Trina and Mel were fast asleep, their combined weight leaning heavily against my arm. It sounded like Mom might have nodded off too, or maybe she'd just gotten really quiet, which she did sometimes. I could only see the top of her shiny blond hair over the seat top, she was nestled down so low. I had been planning to ask her if the area looked much different than when she used to come here every summer, where I pictured her golden tan in a white bathing suit, swimming strongly in the ocean.

Dotted along the expanse of the bridge, turtle-crossing signs showed a mom turtle followed by three little ones. In the Toyota ahead, kids pressed their foreheads and palms against windows, hunting for signs of life.

If I had been looking down too, I would've missed my first glimpse of the town of Wildwood. Low-slung buildings in whites and blues stretched along the coast—a relaxed, mellow look unlike the high-rise casinos of Atlantic City. It was so beachy and inviting. Beyond the buildings rose the uppermost tips of amusement rides. Even from here, I could see the rotation of the Ferris wheel, the tip-top hills of a roller coaster.

Atlantic City had some of that too, but Wildwood was where everybody my age wanted to go—I'd heard of juniors and seniors making the long drive down here after prom, out all night. Trina's older brother, a college sophomore, had come down here for spring break. That sounded much more promising than back home, where, after the way the year had ended, I'd vowed I was done with guys at my school.

Rob-the-too-wet-kisser had started to cling. By month three, he was seeking me out between every class, calling me three times a day. How had it gotten so heavy?

I would see other guys in the hall or after school, hanging out with their own friends. Brian Hunter, for example—whose sculpted body single-handedly made the swim team Speedo about fifty-three points less stupid. After practice he'd join the group lingering out in front of the school. All the girls' eyes would go to him; there would be a palpable pause in the conversation. He just did that, without trying.

Rob would gallop up to me like a puppy who hadn't yet grown into its big paws. He always waited for me, killing time with his sketchbook. At first I'd liked that, his little drawings of hands and eyes and, sometimes, me when I hadn't known he was watching. But after a while, you start to wonder about somebody who does that all the time. Like, don't you have anything better to do?

It had all come to a stuttering halt anyway.

When my swim team won the last finals of the season, I swear Brian Hunter, *the* Brian Hunter, had beamed that white smile at me and said, "Congratulations." He had squeezed my hand, and his cool touch took the breath right out of me. It was a sign. Later that night, when Rob had called, I'd tried to let him down easy.

"I just don't think it's working," I said out of the blue.

"What's not working?" he said. The TV was loud with music in the background.

"You and me," I said, leaving a long pause for him to put it together.

His response was surprised. "Oh. Whoa." I could hear him breathing on the line. The TV had gone quiet. "Why?"

"Why?"

"Yeah, I mean, why? There's got to be a reason."

"I just see you as more like a friend," I said, going for the first thing that came to mind. Somehow I knew he wouldn't have liked to hear, *I'm hot for this guy on the swim team who likes me back.*

All that night, I'd thought about Brian—now that he had kind of made the first move, I would have to make the next.

The next day I put on mascara and wore my hair in a low, messy bun. A sea foam green T-shirt brought out the green in my eyes. All morning it had poured a hot summer rain. I was drenched by the time I got to school, and as I pulled open the front door to the school, there he was right there in the hall—Brian.

My heart sped up. I said, "Hey there, Brian."

Last night, I'd come up with a plan—asking Brian if he wanted to do laps in the pool after school, even though swim practice was over for the year. The whole thing had played out nicely in my head about twenty times. I smiled at him, and this was the part where he was supposed to smile back.

He glanced behind himself, looking for someone. No one was there, so he looked back at me, his brow furrowing into a confused frown.

"Do I know you?" he asked warily.

"Amy," I said quickly. "Amy from the swim team." My face felt hot all of a sudden. Rain dripped from my chin.

"Ohhh," he said, dragging it out. But his look was still blank.

Oh my God. He didn't know who I was.

Panic made a rushing noise in my ears. My mouth was suddenly so dry, my tongue stuck to my teeth. I pulled it free and made a loud smacking sound. He flinched, blinked at me hard.

He was repulsed.

My head shrank down on my shoulders. I looked down and saw that the rain had left dark splotches on my shirt—some of them were black. Oh, no—mascara had run all the way down my face. My wet shoes had started to stink.

I wanted to disappear.

But to Brian, I was already invisible. I had been swimming with this guy for *two years,* yet I'd never even existed in his world.

How come guys like Rob wouldn't leave me alone but Brian couldn't even remember my name?

I shifted to my back foot, giving him more space. "Anyway," I said.

Relief washed over his face. "Have a good summer," he said.

My squishy feet were moving, walking down the hall toward my locker, and I was proud of them for that. "You too," I said.

I had read this whole thing wrong. How could he not even freaking *know* me? This I had to fix. If I could meet someone and try it again, I would do it differently. Be less invisible to the guys who weren't just the desperate, lonely ones who drew pictures of my toes.

As I looked out the car window over the rooftops of Wildwood, I thought, *Maybe here.*

We wound our way into town slowly, the traffic a thick knot of people in no hurry. Along each side of the main drag stood old houses in pastel-mint colors. Most had signs handmade by their owners to name them—THE SHADY LADY, RENEE'S RETREAT, MARGARITAVILLE. Deep, shady porches held bikes, toys, tired wicker furniture that no longer squeaked as you sat on it. Beachgoers returning from a day on the sand walked past us, pink and relaxed.

"God, I can't believe I'm back here," Mom said quietly toward the window, sounding far away. "I never . . ." She trailed off, her voice catching.

Silence stretched on as she stared out the window, her hand covering her mouth. I wondered if she felt carsick, which I did, a little. I knew talking helped me to get my mind off it, so I said to her, "You stayed here all summer when you were a teenager, right?"

Mom sat up a little, ran her hands through her hair. "Yeah," she said, her voice thick but sounding less distant. She turned to face me. "My parents couldn't stay that long, so I stayed with Lynne and her family." She smiled at that thought, her eyes glazing over as she thought back all those years.

"That sounds like fun," I said, keeping my voice upbeat. I wanted to show her I was going to try to make this trip good. Our fighting had gotten to be a daily thing lately, and I was tired. Exhausted.

Mom sighed. "It was great. We'd wake up, roll out of bed, and go to the beach until the sun went down. It was like it was our jobs or something."

"Mmm," I said. That sounded nice.

"Which way?" Tom's impatience finally started to blossom in the traffic. "Right? Left? Which is it?"

Mom leaned up a little. Absently, "Just keep going straight." Her gaze shifted out the side window and she leaned back and slid down again. "Should be two more blocks, on the right."

The motel sat back off the street, and as we swung into the asphalt lot, the first thing I noticed was that the *M* was missing in her blue neon MOTEL sign, so that it read *otel,* sounding French and exotic. Towels were hung to dry over the railing; kids raced each other around the pool. Healthy green potted plants lined the second-floor balcony. The smoky scent of barbecue charcoal wafted in my open window. I smiled.

"Honey, run in and tell Lynne we're here," Mom said to the backseat in general, and since Mel and Trina were still just waking up and since I couldn't wait to get out of the station wagon, I went.

I followed the arrow signs to the office and slipped inside—it was air-conditioned bliss. As my eyes adjusted to the shadows, features took shape—three red chairs from the fifties stood in a neat row, a little waiting area. On the high-countered desk, a black-and-white TV was turned on but muted, the show something I'd seen before but couldn't name. Tidy number two pencils, sharpened, next to a stack of square scratch paper by the phone. An old PC, turned off, with the world's smallest dog napping on top of the monitor. Lemon and fresh mint filled the air. Off in back somewhere, I heard running water stop.

Tinkling ice cubes against glass drew closer, and then Lynne appeared, as tall as Mom but sturdier looking, short salt-and-pepper hair wet from the shower or pool, drinking a glass of iced tea. The running water must've hidden the sound of my entry because I could tell she thought she was alone—and now I was afraid of startling her by saying something.

I thought, maybe I could just wait there in the shadow till she went back to the kitchen; then I'd re-slam the door and shout, "Hel-LO! We're here!"

Then something in the courtyard caught Lynne's gaze and she let out a sigh. She said flatly to herself, "Here comes the sun."

I turned to see. It was Tom, headed our way.

In three quick steps, too fast, before I could think of a single thing to say, he'd crossed the courtyard and flung open the door, filling the office with bright light, the sun like a spotlight exposing me. "Lynne!" he hollered blindly, not seeing her right there. "We're here! Send Amy out!" Then, catching me, "You have bags to carry," before he shut the door. In the dark, everywhere I looked, my eyes could only see a hot yellow square where the door had been.

Silence followed, and I felt like an idiot, still standing there in the dark. "I was just about to call for you," I said. My voice sounded too high.

"Well," Lynne said, and I could hear the smile in her voice. "Call away, kiddo."

I had to laugh. I forgot how silly she could be, in a good way. I cleared my throat, then called in a loud singsongy voice, "Oh, Lyn-ne! Are you here? Is anybody home?"

I heard her reply, "Hello! Who could that be? Amy? Amy, is that you?" Ice cubes tinkled in her glass as she moved, and I saw the outline of her shadow heading toward me.

"It's me!" I said, my fingers feeling blindly out front until I felt her soft arms. She pulled me close in a hug that smelled like fabric softener and soap.

"Nice to see you, Amy. Not that I'm actually *seeing* you just yet."

I laughed. "I'm such a dork," I said.

Lynne said she'd take us up to our room. She and Mom walked ahead, but I was right behind them.

"I wish I had more rooms for you guys," Lynne said.

"One is more than enough," Mom said. "I really appreciate this."

"I thought it was just the four of you, but I can bring up a cot for Mel's friend."

"Tom thought it would be good for the girls to have company. Amy's friend couldn't make it."

My face felt hot. "She had strep," I said, low. "Do we all want to catch strep?" Mom shot me a quick glance over her shoulder.

"Anyway," Lynne said, touching Mom's arm. "I'm glad you're here. Wildwood missed you."

Mom laughed, but there was something strange in the sound—almost nervous, the same laugh that usually filled the kitchen during annual Mother's Day brunches. "So, are we up here?" she asked, pointing to the second floor.

"Yep."

We dragged our luggage up the steps, and when Lynne unlocked the door, I saw Mel's shoulders deflate with disappointment. Mom poked her in the back sharply to keep her quiet.

Inside were two queen-sized beds, divided by a slim nightstand.

We eyed each other, Mel and I, doing the math, thinking, *This could get ugly*. If we put up the cot Lynne mentioned, there'd be zero walking space.

Mom gave us a wink and said, "Lynne, this is great," cheerily. "We are so grateful."

I restrained my eye roll at the big thank-you and flashed Lynne a smile.

"Just holler if you need anything," she said. "Make yourselves at home."

Trina lined up bright bottles on the sill under the massive window. I bent over to read the names—Extreme Anti-Frizz Serum, Glossing Spray, SPF 45 Hair Protector, Stick-Straight Straightening Balm, Big Sexy Hair. She rearranged the order of two identical-looking bottles for no apparent reason.

"You seem a little—" I paused, looking for the right word. "Overprepared."

Trina held a tube called Extreme Deep Treatment Conditioner and looked at me. "What . . . do you . . . mean?" Each word separated by a pause long enough to make me impatient.

"Won't some of these products scientifically negate each other?" I asked. Her head tilted to one side, letting her shiny brown-black bob shift over an eye. This was her I'm-not-getting-you look, so I went on. "Like, can you simultaneously have both big sexy hair *and* stick-straight hair? How does that work? Scientifically speaking?"

Her eyes, the darkest shade of brown and heavily lashed,

darted up to my hair and down again. Someone else might have missed it. "You don't," she said slowly, "use them *together*."

My cheeks reddened. "Oh, I see. You came prepared for several hair occasions."

She blinked slowly, impatient. I was suddenly grateful for my high-necked T-shirt, which hid the splotches coming to my chest.

From the middle of the bed, Mel said, "You don't get it." Her dirty-soled feet were propped up on all the pillows. She watched TV absently, her head upside down over the side of the bed.

"That hurts," I said, "from the girl watching *Knight Rider*." I grabbed a pillow for myself from under Mel's feet. As she rolled over to grab it back, I yanked it away, knocking Trina's bottles onto the floor.

"Goddamn it." Tom thumbed up the volume button on the remote.

Mom's head poked out of the bathroom. "Amy," she said. "Don't start. Don't even think about it."

It wasn't worth explaining. I went out to the balcony and brought the pillow because I felt stupid leaving it after all that. I sat on the floor, watching kids run themselves tired around the pool, till it got too sticky hot to bear. Hearing air conditioners chug all over the courtyard, I walked downstairs and slipped into the cool office.

Lynne was on a stool at the counter-desk, working at the computer. "Hey," she said, smiling.

"You busy?"

She nodded at the screen, trying to look serious. "Very busy. Solitaire."

I laughed, walking around the counter so I could watch over her shoulder. Lynne had always been a game junkie. When Mel and I were little, Mom said, we'd always get sick of playing things before Lynne did.

As Lynne clicked and dragged with the mouse, I noticed an old map laid out flat underneath the glass countertop.

"Is this Wildwood?" I asked, leaning closer to the counter.

Lynne looked down, not sure what I was talking about. "Oh," she said, taking in the map. "That's been there so long I forgot about it." She planted her elbow on the side of the map closest to her.

"Where are we now?"

Lynne took her thumbnail and ran along the beach till she found her street, then slid up a few blocks. "Right here. I should put an X there or something. You know, 'You Are Here,' like in the mall." She ran her thumb over a few streets closer to the beach. "Here's where my parents used to live. Huge place with a wraparound porch."

"Is it still there?"

She shrugged. "Nah. Big hotel there now."

My eyes moved south on the map. "What's down here?" I tapped the next town down.

"Cape May—more pretty houses that are still pretty houses instead of hotels. Oh, and that's where you get the ferry to Delaware."

"What's that?" I pointed to a spot far up north, almost covered by her elbow.

"A lighthouse."

"Ooh, that'd be neat to see."

Lynne shifted, leaning more heavily on her elbow. "Nah, stay away from there. It's not much to see. Lots of wilderness and swampland, and the neighborhood leading up to it is kind of rough."

"I can hold my own," I said jokingly, flexing my muscles.

She didn't laugh. "I'm serious, Amy. Look, the streets are numbered north to south—you stay out of anything north of Twentieth Street."

I shrugged. "What's over there?" I asked, pointing to the area covered by her forearm.

"More swamps," she said.

"Swamps, gangs, shady neighborhoods—not to be rude, but exactly why do people vacation here?"

Lynne laughed, a loud howl, and swatted me on the butt. "They come here for my sparkling company," she said. We both looked up as the door opened. Mom stuck her head in. "I'm going to grab hoagies for dinner," she said.

"Why don't you go walk with your mom?" Lynne said. "Leave this old lady to her solitaire."

Mom nodded to me, and I walked with her out of the courtyard. The sun had worked its way down closer to the horizon, and the sky was purplish. I could smell salt water in the air. We made our way out to the sidewalk in silence.

"Dad didn't like coming down here?" I said, just to say something. Mom shrugged. "I guess not."

"I think it would be romantic."

We walked in step, me taking long strides to keep pace with her. Finally she said, "He wasn't into it. He's not much of a relaxer."

I laughed. Dad's condo storage space overflowed with busy oddities. Paintball guns and protective eyewear, splotched with hot pink hits. Rock-climbing ropes, hopelessly knotted. Chrome rims too small to fit his SUV. A CPR dummy, golf clubs with hand-knit socks on their heads—both from a yard sale, neither one used. Last time we'd spent the weekend together, we'd gone bowling, and I'd sat down in the plastic scoop chair next to his and seen that that my muscular thighs had grown to be as thick as his, maybe thicker, and spent the rest of the night standing.

"No, not so much," I said.

Belly's Hoagie Hut smelled like fresh-baked rolls and sweet oregano. Mom ordered a bunch of Italian hoagies, and we waited while a heavyset guy, likely Belly-the-Hut himself, sliced the lunch meat with a noisy, old-fashioned slicer.

"So would you and Lynne just go to the beach? What else would you do?"

"Swim," Mom said. "My arms ached at the end of the day."

Swimming was one thing we had in common. Back in high school, Mom had made it to the Pennsylvania State Championships three years in a row.

"I already miss swim team," I said.

"It's good for you to have some time off."

I closed my eyes briefly, hating when she did that—dissuaded me from working too hard. Her subconscious was probably telling her to do that since I was born two months premature—I think she was always afraid I might break. I guess I kind of was too. Doctors always assured me that I was in perfect condition and that nothing was wrong with my heart, but secretly I knew that being two months early *changed things.* I'd even seen it once as a kid, on a PBS documentary that followed a group of premature babies into their teen years—where they were sicker, weaker than their peers. Pale-skinned and forever with a doctor's note excusing them from gym class, that's how I knew I'd end up if I ever stopped training so hard.

"I don't need any time off," I said. I knew it sounded cocky, but so what? I was good. One of the two best on the varsity swim team—and that was as a sophomore. After some practice over the summer, I knew next year I would top that.

"I know, Aim," she said. She put a warm hand on my shoulder; it was already kind of warm in the shop, and I fought the urge to shake it off. She felt me stiffen and stepped to the counter to check on the order. "These look like the hoagies we got for your birthdays."

Our birthdays. Mel and I were eleven months apart, and that meant that for half of the months of April and May, Mel and I were the same exact age. This year she'd turned fifteen April fifteenth, and

I'd hurried through the thirty days till I turned sixteen. Somewhere in between our birthdays, Mom would throw a joint birthday party—it worked when we were younger, but now, Mel's friends, suspicious-eyed and on their way somewhere better, kept a distance from mine, all girls, who gave me gifts tied with matching ribbon.

The whole thing confused most people, who were left thinking we must be fraternal twins. Me as the smart one and Mel as the pretty one.

The deli cashier handed me a paper bag, already showing the promising wet stains of drippy oil and vinegar. On the way back, Mom hummed "Under the Boardwalk" and I buried my nose in the bag, breathing deep the smells of spicy ham and crusty bread. Maybe the situation with Mel wasn't so bad. For ten more months I would have sixteen to myself.

There were a few things that made it hard to sleep that night.

Thing one: two Diet Pepsis with dinner. Bad idea.

Thing two: Mel and Trina had each claimed one side of the bed. That left the middle for me, since there was really no room for the cot.

Thing three: I couldn't get Jason, Mel's friend with cancer, off my mind. Before bed, I'd snuck a quick read of her postcard, which Mel had left on the nightstand: *Dear J: Wanted to give you a look at this weird town we passed thru today—see what you're not missing??? Seriously, wish you could be here anyway. Hang in there, cutie. Trina sends love too. XO, Melvin.*

Although I'd never met him, I thought about Jason a lot. For the last year and a half, I'd get updates from Mel. Hearing her come home from school, I'd slip out from my room. She'd be sitting Indian style in front of the TV, watching *People's Court*. At a commercial, I'd ask, "How was school?"

"Not good," Mel would say, the little corners of her pink mouth pulled down.

Or, "He's starting to lose his hair."

And about him throwing up in the bathroom sometimes but not wanting to go to the nurse's office because even just sitting in class was better than being in the hospital.

It seemed unfair—tragedy picking this one guy at random, missing me by just *this much*. And as I lay there in bed, listening to Mel and Trina breathe deep on either side of me, I felt like a jerk. Here I was, healthy, normal—and miserable. People like Jason probably hated ungrateful people like me.

Tomorrow could be the day I started to change all that.

No more fighting with Tom about insults he tossed my way. Resisting his bait would be hard, but I could do that.

I could lay off Mel, too, and Mom while I was at it.

These three days down here could be a new start to all of it.

I sat up in bed so I could see myself in the dresser mirror to see if I looked as different as I felt. The mirror was tilted weird, so I had to get up on my knees, and even then I could only see the top of my forehead. But yes, I thought, that part *did* look more Zen.

And that's when I noticed him—a guy standing down by the pool in the courtyard. Slim, with the broad shoulders of a swimmer, his hands resting in the front pockets of his windbreaker. I swear, I thought he was looking right up at my dark window. Could he see me in here, staring right back at him? That thought startled me. But he didn't even look away as I reached over Trina, dead asleep, and jerked the blinds closed.

CHAPTER *Three*

THE NEXT MORNING, I MADE COFFEE FOR MOM AND TOM AND, surprisingly, Trina, in the miniature Mr. Coffee in the room. Not hard at all. I waited till last shift in the bathroom, and even though there were no clean towels left, I didn't complain once.

I was so proud of myself.

Mom seemed to notice, too. As we stepped out on the balcony to go to the beach, she softly gathered my hair in a loose ponytail and said, "Did you remember to bring a barrette, hon?" I already had one in my bag, but I went inside and grabbed another one just to make nice.

That's when I saw him. The guy from last night was down in the courtyard. The little hairs on my arms stood up. He was sitting on the edge of the pool, his feet in the water, while two little kids swam a dog-paddle race that was all splashes and yelling. He was laughing too. Water droplets clung to his arms; I could see the outlines of nice biceps. I licked my lips and shifted my shoulders back, put on my sunglasses, glad for the really dark lenses. I walked down the steps slowly behind everybody else.

He glanced up our way, still smiling. I managed to smile back. His smile widened, watching me.

"I won! I won!" one of the boys yelled.

"*I* won!" the other boy shouted.

Both kids looked at their judge, hopeful. I felt a tingling sensation in my toes, flattered that their judge was officially busted not paying attention. "That was a tie," he finally ruled.

"*I* won," they both said again.

The guy tilted his head to me. "Can I get a second opinion?" he called.

Those eyes, light blue like winter sky. My pulse quickened. "Most definitely a tie," I said, laughing, sounding cool.

The first boy pounded the water. "No fair!"

"Do over!" the other kid yelled.

"Do overs suck."

We both laughed.

Just then, Tom's voice called, "Where is she?" from the front gate. I hadn't realized how far behind I'd fallen. I quickened my step to catch up, trying not to feel too disappointed that I was leaving yummy bicep boy behind.

Until that day, I'd had no idea how serious some people could be about the beach. Wildwood people were *those* kind of people. They set up base camp on a scale equal to people climbing Mount Everest.

They brought *supplies.*

Old bed comforters laid out side by side, shoes weighting down each corner. Coolers on wheels with pull handles, filled with lunch meat hoagies, juice boxes, illegal wine coolers. One small battery-powered TV playing a soap opera. Old boom boxes, antennas outstretched and fire hot from the sun, a different station competing for attention from every blanket.

I lay down, squiggling and shifting around till I felt the sand grains form a cozy outline for my body, meeting every inch of my spine. The goose bumps were gone, but so far this day was turning a corner to something good. That guy, he had definitely noticed me—I had seen that much. I focused on that thought, struggling to stay coolly unfazed by the discussion taking place next to me.

"They can grow to be forty feet in diameter," Tom was saying loudly over the crashing waves. "The stingers alone have been known to kill. Really."

A disgusted laugh from Trina. "Please."

"Well, if not kill, then paralyze," he said, holding his ground. "The jellyfish stingers, they actually pass electrical shocks that zap your central nervous system. Suddenly, you can't move your limbs." Tom demonstrated by freezing his meaty-muscled arms, already pinkish from the sun. His legs jutted out straight from his beach chair, too close to my face, his small feet pink-bottomed like a baby's.

"Well, I'm not going in," Mel said, folding up her long, lean legs and arms, as though someone would drag her into the ocean by one of them.

Tom didn't swim. Though he never said so, I thought he might not know how. So every vacation he did this kind of thing. Last time it was riptides—how they can suck you away, right off your feet, splash, goodbye. Dirty syringes washing up on the beach, pricking your skin as you paddled along, infecting you with AIDS or something—that had been another time. It was like before every vacation, Tom went to the local bookstore and grabbed the last copy of the *How-to-Terrify-Your-Stepdaughters Times*.

I stared out at the crisp silvery greenness of the ocean. Tom had us where he wanted us, here on the beach.

I tried to catch Mel's eye to see if she had put this together, but she was already lying down, maybe asleep, her body coated in a sheen of sweat, badly in need of a cool dip. Both of us, we loved the water. Maybe it came from growing up surrounded by Mom's collection of mermaid things—key chains, Christmas ornaments, a hand-painted mug Mom drank coffee from each morning. Little mermaids everywhere we looked. They had crept into our heads and taken hold.

Goose bumps rose as it hit me that I had the nerve to do something different.

I tried to be nonchalant as I pushed myself up from the sand and readjusted my swimsuit, squaring my shoulders.

"I'm going in," I said.

Mel propped herself up on an elbow and squinted at me

through the sunlight. As kids, we'd spend whole days in the ocean at Sea Isle City. We'd be so water-pruned at the end of the day, we'd huddle close with cups of cherry water ice and let Mom tease us about how she was afraid our fingers would never de-wrinkle again.

But that was then.

Now she just lay back down and rested the crook of her arm over her eyes.

So I turned and headed for the water and didn't look back once. I figured Tom was keeping an eye on me. I just fixed my eyes on the foamy waves breaking out at sea and walked.

It was warmer than I expected—one of those days where if you stood still in the shallows too long, your feet would get buried, and soon you'd be up to your calves in soft quicksand that didn't want to let go. I waded out into shoulder-high water before I even knew it, to the place the waves swelled up but didn't break. That's when I finally took a quick peek at the beach, where all of them back on our blanket looked so small, just like everyone else.

The tide was pulling strongly to the south, so I turned north and started swimming into it. The familiar freestyle form told my muscles what to do, and I sliced through the water quickly, wondering what the guy from the pool might be doing back at the motel. Who was he? What if he was leaving that day and I never got a chance to find out? The way he'd looked at me gave me the feeling that he could be wondering the same thing about me. If I didn't want to keep pulling in guys like Rob—who was just like my two other quasi boyfriends before him, one of whom Reb still referred to as Hairy Steve—this guy was the perfect opportunity to try. To trade up a league.

My arms were ready to switch to something new. I started the butterfly into the swift current. I could feel my upper arms and chest muscles working hard, propelling me forward, my heartbeat pounding strongly in my chest.

I always thought this was the showiest stroke. Freeze-framed for a second above the water, it was one of swimming's most perfect "look-at-me" moves. Mom could do it amazingly well—she swam as effortlessly as she walked. We were at the apartment complex's pool once, and she was doing laps, and I remembered it hitting me—*That kind of beauty, it's in my genes.*

And it was. But there was something else in my genes too—my nearly two-month-premature heart. Right after a race on swim team, I would stand dripping by the poolside, fighting to grab ahold of my breathing, a little worried that this time I'd strained too hard. Hunched over, hands on my knees, swallowing lungfuls of air, I pictured the sad little galloping organ in my chest—probably just the size of a peach and bruised like that too. And if that sounds bad, listen to this: in deep water the panic got even worse. Down below eight feet, the pressure on my chest became powerful and, I thought, deadly. I'd find myself darting for the top before my heart decided to stop working.

So that was the secret of my swimming strength. I was powered by pure fear. Swim team was the one thing I'd really stuck with through school. I was good at it, maybe because I'd never given *not* being good at it much consideration. So when I turned out to be not so good at other things, I learned to master the fine art of bailing. Like debate team, which had been too good-mannerly. (*And* they docked points for interrupting.) Same thing for soccer—if I felt like sailing down the field by myself with the ball, why was that wrong? So I'd bailed on soccer. Bailing was fine. *That* was in my blood too, from my dad. It was the one thing he and I had in common. Mel got his leanness, his blondness, his golden-tanness, his everything-goodness. I got his good flaking skills.

Technically, I could stick to things when I wanted to. Like swimming. And if I met a guy like the one at the pool and could learn to get him to like me back, I was sure I could stick with him too. So happily.

My arms had started to burn, from the sun or from the pounding strokes. Although I'd gone steadily into the tide, when I finally got out of the water, I was easily half a mile up shore from where I'd stepped into the sea. Finding our blanket required an extensive analysis of baby-oiled flesh—I trekked through blankets, thinking: *No, too chunky, not them, too Italian, too G-stringed.*

By the time I got to familiar territory, my hair had dried, each strand curling its own way, the tip of my nose like leather, sea salt crusted at the corners of my mouth. This was what it must be like to be lost in the desert.

Ahead I spotted an oasis.

Tall and cool, her linen shirt parachuting with a breeze that I couldn't even feel, my mother was standing, staring at the ocean. Behind her on the blanket, propped up on his elbows, was Tom. He was squinting painfully into the sun, watching Mom, so taken by her, I swear he wasn't even breathing.

I wanted someone to look at me that way. If I had to trade everything I had in the world for it, I would've at that moment.

I sank to my knees on the blanket. And I thought, maybe there were more similarities between Mom and me than swimming. Maybe I had her appeal too. I tried it. "I would kill for a lemonade right now," waiting to see if Tom volunteered.

Tom looked away from Mom at me. "That's not a bad idea." He started reaching for his shoes.

I smiled. Maybe I did have it. And maybe I'd made a connection this morning with the coffee thing—just a little thing, but a step.

Tom pulled his wallet out of his shoe, withdrew a five, and tossed it to me. "I'll have a large," he said.

Stung, I took the cash, slipped on my T-shirt, and started to walk.

The trek back to the boardwalk was like one of those impossibly long journeys from the Bible. That stretch of scorching sand was famous for breaking people or tiring them so much they'd abandon good stuff along the trail. Cheap beach chairs, foam coolers, a Phillies cap—flotsam left behind to make the trip more bearable.

When I came up the steps, winded, I was standing by the

games of chance. Enormous wheels with spades, hearts, clubs, and diamonds; shoot your water gun into the clown's gaping mouth to fill and burst a balloon; knock cans off a milk jug with a giant softball. They all seemed so easy but really weren't.

All these guys in the softball-milk-jug-ripoff booth, they were all looking down the boardwalk at someone approaching. So I looked too. It was a girl, of course. I guess the way she walked was what I noticed first because it was so determined and casual at the same time. Like, *I've got somewhere to go, but I know they'll wait for me.* And then there was the hair, a shade of brown that reflected light like a mirror. A beautiful, angled face looked lost in thought somewhere.

As she neared, the booth guys yelled hellos, and she gave a casual wave. "Hey, Curt, Mike, what's going on." More a statement than a question.

"Free throw?" shouted the darker guy, who was a kind of outdoorsy handsome they didn't make back home in Philly.

"Yeah, take a free throw!" called the other one.

She smiled at them as she passed. "Gotta run," she said, her straw sandals with little blue ribbon ties around the ankle not missing a beat. She just breezed right by, her denim skirt pulled taut with each long stride, her spaghetti strap top showing a glimpse of the small of her back.

The lemonade stand was right next to their booth. I darted up to it quickly and ordered two large drinks, wishing I'd brought a barrette and a pair of shorts.

Next to me, the guys stared blankly out into the crowd. I waited for them to say, "Free throw?" to me as I stood there twisting straw papers and waiting for my order. They didn't.

So finally I said nicely to the girl behind the counter, "Can I just get a cup holder when you have a sec?" as she set two buckets of fluorescent yellow lemon-flavored beverage in front of me.

"All out," she said.

I rolled my eyes and stacked one cup on top of the other. I had to hold the top with my chin. Back on the beach, my chest damp from the cups sloshing around, I looked for our blanket. What caught my eye was Tom: he and my mom were kissing deeply like teenagers. He held her face in both hands, oblivious to everything, including me, as I walked up and set the lemonades in the sand at his feet.

"I got one for Mom too. And I got you guys the extra-long straws," I said, wedging them between the cups. No response. I couldn't even look at them. "And here's your change. I'll just, uh, leave it."

NO LIFEGUARD ON DUTY.

WELCOME TO OUR OOL. (PLEASE NOTICE WE LEFT THE "PEE" OUT.)

When we got back to the motel, I scanned the pool quickly for the guy from earlier, but he wasn't there. The blue water would've called my name anyway, even if Tom hadn't suggested we go swimming. He led Mom up the stairs by her hand, and we dropped our bags and towels as if gravity had suddenly gotten heavier and slid into the pool.

Underneath the water, everything had soft edges. My legs, even, looked like tan flippers with Revlon Fire and Ice dotted at the tips. I flexed-pointed flexed-pointed and swished my elbows, just messing around. That was what I was doing as Mel swam toward me, her hair a billowing blond trail, holding up the penny we were scouring the pool floor for—her idea, a flashback to what we'd do to kill time at the pool when we were growing up. She always found the coin effortlessly. Her luck worked that way.

Trina lay drip-drying at the pool's rim, as though turning her skin that delicious golden color today had exhausted her completely.

I was underwater when suddenly he appeared. Standing in the corner, tan and relaxed and at home, he put on swimmer's goggles and slid under the water's surface. One of my friends from swimming had once said that I looked pretty with wet hair, that it brought out my cheekbones or something, so as Mel and I stood at the pool's edge with our eyes closed to throw the penny in again, I thought I could feel him watching me, and I felt a shiver run through me. I wanted him to notice the graceful muscles of my back, my calves. Thrill sped up my pulse. Maybe he was thinking I was amazing, wishing someone like me would notice someone like him.

There was a small splash, then a bigger splash of Mel diving in.

Too fast, showing off, I raised my arms and blindly thrust toward the water, knowing right away it was all wrong. I opened my eyes just as my chin scraped the concrete bottom, rattling my teeth—but my hand, it grabbed the dark spot I saw from the corner of my eye. I had gotten the penny.

I broke the surface, touching the small patch of rough skin and feeling the sting that surely meant at least a little blood.

"Are you okay?" he asked, breaking the surface right in front of me. He took my hand away from my chin to see, and, shocked by the sting and by his touch, I let the penny slip between my fingers. So close, his brow furrowed, blue eyes studying my injury, dark hair still sleeked back from his fast swim. "Just a scrape," he said. "People do it here all the time—it's shallower than it looks. Keep swimming—the chlorine is good for it."

I lowered myself to nose deep into the water, studying the way the late-afternoon sunlight made highlights on the droplets on his upper back. He was beautiful, smooth skin and broad shoulders. I could picture him poolside at one of my swim meets, waving to me, cheering me on, everyone wondering, *Who is that guy?* Suddenly I felt a swish in the water next to me. Mel surfaced right then with the penny.

"Mine again," she said, her eyes quickly flashing to the guy. I met his eyes and he looked at me, like he half expected me to correct her—*No, I found it first*—but I just let her have the moment. Or at least let her *think* she had the moment. Figuring it out, the guy bit his lip, hiding the hint of a smile.

It was almost like I could hear Mel's motor start. "So, I don't know what I'm going to do," Melissa said to Trina, like they'd been mid-conversation. "I have to get those letters to some office—city something, city council? Does that sound right? And they want them by, like, next week."

Trina shrugged at Mel. "I don't understand"—flipping over lazily—"why you bother with that crap."

Mel shook her head. Then, to clarify, she looked at the guy and said, "I'm doing this petition thing to help underprivileged kids."

The goggles had left little pink half circles under his eyes. He looked from me to her, then said warily, "Like, for scholarships or something?"

"Actually," she said, "it's to build a summer camp for them."

"Oh," he said. He looked at me to see if I was impressed. I blew bubbles out of my nose into the water.

"Who's the petition for?" he asked.

Mel paused a beat to dip her hair back in the water, making it sleek against her head. Looking back at him, she said, "Habitat for Humanity."

His brow furrowed a little. "They build houses for the poor."

"And now they'll build a summer camp too."

"But shouldn't you be collecting *donations* or something instead of signatures?" he asked.

"Why?"

"I don't know," he said, folding his arms in front of him. "Aren't petitions for stuff like gun control? Gay marriage? Stuff people have clashing opinions about."

He looked at me.

I nodded, my mind far away, wondering if having this guy by my side after a swim meet next season would catch Brian's eye. Make him realize what he'd missed. Competitiveness like that, I knew guys like Brian had it.

He went on. "So who's *against* a camp for poor kids?" My laugh caught me by surprise, coming out as a burst of air bubbles underwater. Mel headed for the side of the pool, in no hurry.

His brow furrowed adorably. "Wait," he said, looking at her. "You're making this up."

Mel's eyes went squinty; she was taken aback.

"Aren't you?" he said. "There is no petition, is there?"

"There is," Mel said, hiking herself up on the edge of the pool. "But I guess you're not signing it."

"Show it to me."

Mel lowered her brows. "What do you have against poor people anyway?" she said, an edge to her voice now. Then to me and Trina, "C'mon, it's time to go up." Trina slowly sat up, started gathering towels, bags. Mel wrapped a thick towel low around her hips so just her tan little toes showed at the bottom.

I didn't budge and it took Melissa several seconds to realize this.

"Fine. Miss dinner if you want."

I ducked underwater and swam to the far end of the pool in one single breath, hoping he would follow. And he did. When he surfaced, he was so close I could smell his cinnamon chewing gum. His wet eyelashes were jet black around intense eyes, the color of water. I didn't want to look away but felt like I had to, or else he'd know how much I liked him.

"So am I the crazy one?" he asked.

I laughed, trying to break the tension. "We're all a little crazy," I said, the new, nice me talking. "Besides, crazy is good. Do you have any more gum?"

"Last piece," he said. He took the gum out of his mouth, showing it to me.

I pretended to admire it. "You do good work," I said. He laughed and stuck it back in his mouth, then ran a hand through his hair quickly. Was he nervous? He put on his goggles and dove downward. Seconds later, he surfaced with the penny. He pointed at me, then at the side of the pool.

"Uh-oh," I said, laughing.

His eyebrows raised and lowered comically. "Afraid?"

"Oh God. I think I'm only allowed to have one fourth-grade flashback a day."

"You fear the penny hunt," he said in a creaky old voice, faking like he was reading a crystal ball. In the goggles, he looked so goofy I had to laugh. He still kept it up. "You're not a sporting loser."

"Oh?" I could see little blue outlines of myself in his lenses; the wet hair was working, thank God. "Who says I would lose?"

He smiled wickedly. All at once, we both hoisted ourselves up onto the edge, cool pool water streaming off us in rivulets. He handed me the coin. "Your toss."

How sweet. Then I pointed at his goggles. "Cheating."

He slid them down around his neck. "I forgot. If you're blind, I'm blind."

"Ready?" He gave me a quick nod, and I launched the penny overhead. "One, two—three!"

He was fast. He dove in shallow like me, and we both shot quickly to the other end. Chalky white pool bottom stretched out in front of me. No sign of the penny. I glanced over and saw the fuzzy outline of him still searching too. Then I saw him pause and I followed his gaze. The penny. It was on the second step from the bottom.

He swam toward it fast, and I chased, hearing the watery sound of my excited scream. Then, just before he got to the step, he reversed his arm stroke to bring himself to a halt, and my momentum carried me forward into him. He paused a beat to give me a chance to get the penny. This guy was so sweet, I did something that came naturally—I took his hand and moved it toward the penny to pick it up. When we surfaced, we were both breathing hard, trying to stop smiling.

"The steps are technically out-of-bounds anyway," he said. "I believe that makes grounds for a do over."

I laughed. "Do overs suck."

Little whiskers on his cheeks and chin made me want to touch his face. He caught me looking. "Let's just swim," he said.

We started in lazy circles, far from each other, but soon found ourselves in the deep end. Through my fuzzy eyes I saw he'd put his goggles back on, so I waved, and he waved back. I pushed off the wall, showing off, doing a flip underwater that left my hair floating crazy above me. He pushed off and came near, touching my hair. Though I couldn't see it clearly, I thought of his chin stubble and pictured my lips pressing against it. To kiss a guy like him, there would be none of Rob's saliva bath. None of Hairy Steve's sweaty hands.

When I broke for a quick breath, I heard Tom calling my name, and I dove under again, hoping he would go away. But the last thing I needed was him coming down and ruining this for me, so I headed back up.

He surfaced right after me. "Are you here tomorrow?"

I felt little happy things doing a dance in my stomach, and I tried to sound casual, climbing out of the pool and grabbing my towel. "Yes. Are you?"

He smiled. "I'm always here."

I headed for the steps, and I'd rounded the corner, passed the office, and made it just two steps up to the second floor when Tom appeared in front of me.

"Are you ready for dinner?" he said. Comb tracks showed in his hair, fresh from the shower.

"I'll be quick," I said.

"I think you should go like that," he said, getting loud, louder. "I hear you're down here flirting with some guy, so why should we have to wait for you while you fuck off?"

I tried to control my cringe, worrying that the guy—I suddenly realized, I didn't even know his name—might hear. My teeth clenched and I stared hard at Tom's chin, where I could see a dot of blood scabbing over from his shave. I tried to focus on that, calm. "You heard wrong. I was just swimming. I said I'll be fast." I should've stopped there, but I didn't. "Besides, it won't kill you to wait." I resisted the urge to poke his belly, which had grown bigger in the last two years.

He caught my eyes and put together the insult. Laughed, mean. Then, loudly, "If only your brain was half as smart as that mouth of yours."

Stupid boldness took me. "I'd still be smarter than your sorry ass," I said, trying to slip past him on the steps.

Wrong answer, and I knew it, so I didn't fight much as Tom grabbed my arm, the pressure from his fingers causing white outlines on my sunburn. "You'll be fine in what you're wearing. Nobody looks at you," he said. "Let's go to the car."

I looked down at my bathing suit, still dripping water. The towel around me had a picture of a koala bear holding a Foster's Lager—"It's Australian for beer, mate!" In my backpack, I had a T-shirt, lip gloss, and a barrette, which I used to hold back my hair in the station wagon's window mirror. Damp like this, I knew I'd freeze in an air-conditioned restaurant, but there was no way out and I was determined not to show Tom that I really cared. I met the amused gaze of Trina as she and Mel came down the steps, both looking clean and cute, smelling like hotel soap. I silently envied their dry hair and eyed the gray sweatshirt Mel had tied around her waist but didn't ask for it. Mom came down last. Chic in black linen and looking younger from the day's sun. She smiled at me over the backseat. "You were always like a fish. Even when you were little, I could never get you out of the water."

It was rare to hear her mention me being younger, when we were really pretty broke and at times scared to death, worrying that things would never be good again after she and Dad broke up. So I just shut up and held that thought in my head for a while—me as a fish, skimming through the depths—instead of telling her I wasn't sitting here in my swimsuit by choice.

After dinner, I changed, and since I didn't see the pool guy any-where around, I headed toward the strip of games and shops that lined the beach. If Rebecca had been here, it would've felt more like an adventure, but as it was, I trailed behind Melissa and Trina, half to annoy them but half out of boredom, too.

The boardwalks that lined the Jersey shores all had the same smell. Wood wet by the heavy salt air smells like a campfire, thick and aged. Throngs of sunburned people streamed each way, and we merged with them—Mel, with her top two fly buttons open, letting the henna tattoo around her navel dry. It was the size of a drink lid—a wavy sunburst surrounding her outie belly button.

"Is she going to follow us all night?" Trina said, loud enough for me to hear.

Mel shrugged. "We must be fascinating."

"Obviously."

Mel laughed. With sarcasm, she said, "Aw, be nice. She didn't have a friend to bring along."

"Shouldn't she be out with her boyfriend?"

"The boyfriend who dumped her?"

"Not that it matters what you think, but I dumped him, losers," I said.

"Did you hear something?" Trina said.

Mel shook her head no. And I almost missed it as they quickly darted down the steps to the beach, which was pitch-black and probably so cold. I followed, just to torture them some more.

Though not much time had passed, the sand felt so different—soothing the same feet it scalded earlier. I felt funny, hot but freezing, too. What was that rushing sound filling my ears? Blood pumping? It suddenly hit me how perfect it would be to take this exact walk with the pool boy. The dark made you hyperaware, like a cat in a black room, every sense heightened. I thought, *I like this feeling.*

Huge waves had washed big jellyfish up onto the shore. Seaweed, too. Carrying one shoe in each hand, arms folded around myself to shake off the sunburn chills, I followed Mel and Trina's footprints and took inventory of what I stepped over— cracked shell, plastic bucket handle, Milky Way wrapper. Was that . . . what? Part of a sombrero? Up ahead they were stopped, looking down at something. I caught up.

"Ew," Mel said, taking a step back.

The overturned horseshoe crab was still alive, its foot-long needle tail pointing back toward the ocean, where it wanted to go. I crouched down and balanced on the balls of my feet, wanting to flip it over and give it a good shove back to sea. Its legs, pointed upward, scrambled to grab something to give it the leverage to turn over, and I saw how pretty the moonlight was, shining on its shell. No matter how much he struggled, he'd never be able to turn over, because he wasn't made like that.

One little push, even with my shoe, that'd be enough. But I couldn't, so I just stared.

Above me I heard a muffled whisper and laugh, and a moment before it happened, somewhere deep inside the pit of my stomach, I knew what Trina was about to do. My arm muscles tensed as I resisted, reaching out to break my fall. Her sharp shove against my back tipped me over, and my knee landed hard on the crab's underbelly. Its legs reflexively curled, grabbing my knee as I crunched through its shell. It was done before I could stop it.

"Whoa, you killed it," Mel said softly.

I wasn't sure if she meant me or Trina, although technically it had been me. I knew enough to know I couldn't hit Trina like I wanted to, so instead I stood and shoved Melissa, hard. She quick-stepped toward the water to get out of my path. And I just kept walking, heading north, picking up the pace once I was sure I was out of their line of sight, my walk turning into an all-out run that would take me somewhere far away from all this.

CHAPTER *Four*

THE BALLS OF MY FEET POUNDED INTO THE SAND—IT FELT GOOD
to hit something hard.

I almost hoped I'd cross paths with a wannabe mugger or
rapist; I surged with the urge to pummel someone with all the
energy stored in my muscles. I ran with slamming steps that
would've echoed on any ground other than sand, hands fisted,
daring to be messed with.

Fighting chunks of memories, old stuff.

How once I told Mom I was going to get my butt kicked after
school, and she still made me go, promising to call the principal
and intervene. How long that school day felt. I'd held my breath
every time the overhead speaker crackled, wishing for my name to
be called, which it never was, while a tall, acne-scarred girl stared
at me dead-eyed from across the classroom.

Me in a mermaid Halloween costume, age seven.

Pink tongues from cherry water ice.

Squeezing in the front seat of the old car, me, Mom, and Mel, perfect because it fit the three of us on the wide bench seat, one two three, like the tiny pearls on Mom's favorite old necklace.

A new circle of little cuts radiated outward on my kneecap like a sunburst; they stung and burned as I splashed through salt water.

I tuned all that out. And I just ran.

Humidity curls made crazy loops that stuck to my face. The back of my sweaty shirt clung like skin.

At the northmost end of the boardwalk where a rock jetty interrupted the sand, a slim lighthouse sat out at the end. Lynne had been right—it wasn't much to see. Up at this end of town, the shops and piers full of rides were replaced by quiet, run-down hotels left behind thirty years ago when the action moved south. Out of breath and wary from Lynne's warning, I slowed to a walk and headed up to the boardwalk, then down into the little town of North Wildwood, where the streets were quiet and deserted.

The lonely roads started to quiet the pounding in my head, and since the place looked fine, not scary—just kind of *normal*— I kept walking, looking for something that would tell me what to do next.

The street ended at a rural highway, its blackness yawning back at me from both directions.

A dead end. Perfect.

I looked up at the road sign—it said FIRST STREET. Uh-oh. That was *way* north of Twentieth Street.

I had to sit down on the curb. Laughter, crazy laughter,

bubbled up and out, and I knew how I must look to all the sleepy houses around me. Dark windows stared at me, saying, "Now what?"

I gathered my hair and tied it into a knot at the base of my neck, letting the night wind dry the sweat. Slowly it started to set in on me, the stupidity of coming this far, so late and alone—it started to fill my mind in a steady drumbeat. If this place had once been as bad as Lynne still thought it was, a few pockets were probably still pretty bad. I could easily stumble across some of that on the way back.

I rested my face in my hands, suddenly very tired. Couldn't somebody carry me home? Wouldn't it be perfect if the pool guy happened to be driving by right now, and he could pick me up and drop me off, and maybe we'd stop for Dairy Queen along the way?

Just then, a string of cars zoomed past, and by the light of their headlights, I caught a glimpse of a roadside sign that'd been hidden by darkness before. Once the road cleared, I was up on my feet and across the highway, bare feet skimming across black-top, in six, seven, eight quick steps to get a closer look.

I wasn't sure how old the sign was, but the broad black brush-strokes had faded and started to peel. And I could hardly believe my eyes.

It was the image of a bombshell of a woman from the waist up, in a bikini top made to look like seashells, her hair set in plump pin curls, ruby red lips pouting over a toothpaste smile— but from the waist down, she was a single glittering fin.

A mermaid.

The scales were actual individual blue, green, and silver sequins, nailed to the billboard one by one, painstakingly. The years had removed a few, but the overall effect was still breathtaking.

A line read: THEY REALLY DO EXIST!

MERMAID PARK, JUST 1/2 MILE AHEAD.

I set a quick pace for the park.

I came to a single-lane road that carved a path back through the woods. Goose bumps rose as I read the huge sign in front of me: MERMAID PARK. I headed down the road into the woods, the crickets making a lush backdrop for my creeping. Leaves rustled in the wind. My throat was tight and dry as I swallowed, and I was suddenly aware of how fast my breathing had become.

Ahead was the park entrance. I ducked under a single string of white twinkle lights that made a sad arc over the wooden gate and was relieved to discover that the ticket booth was empty and dark—I slipped under the turnstile on my hands and knees and went to see what was inside.

Without meaning to, I let out a soft gasp when I saw it.

The entire park lay beneath me, flooded in cool blue light. It was like a builder had taken away a giant ice-cream scoop of earth and in the concave cavity that remained had built an amphitheater. Thirty rows of bleachers were built into the hillside, half circling center stage.

Except it wasn't a stage at all.

It was a massive aquarium, a blue-green gem.

I slid into the top row of bleachers, my knees weak.

Suddenly tinny calypso music burst from the speakers, startling me. A mermaid swam into view inside the tank. I must have come in on her private rehearsal.

She quickly began circling the tank, swimming strong, using just her arms and a swift thrust with her legs, which from waist to tiptoes were bound together in a single sequined mermaid fin. She moved gracefully to the beat, arms arcing skillfully, bringing her to a stop in the middle of the tank. With a curve of her back and an effortless swish of her fin, she drew three quick backward flips in the water.

I couldn't look away.

Holding her breath for well over thirty seconds now, she didn't head to the surface like I'd expected. She darted behind a giant oyster shell and emerged fast, spiraling tightly and dizzyingly, the white wideness of her smile catching the light on each turn. I blinked. How she glowed and shimmered, how she lasted for so long without air—how could all this really be happening? Was it magic somehow?

She was moving with power but something else, too. Joy. Like ballet underwater, unconfined by gravity. Moving like water, circling, cycling, in a way I had never thought of before. Part of the current instead of just slicing through it.

As the last drumbeats of the song faded, she darted out of view, and after a minute, the lights clicked off. She must be done.

My shoulders lowered and I drew air in deeply and hungrily. The thought hit me that maybe I was dreaming.

I went down the bleachers to touch the aquarium and make sure it was real. Just getting closer to it, I could feel my heartbeat slow, calm.

When I touched the glass, I found it was as warm as the night. Now that the lights were out, the water was pitch-dark and reflecting me like a mirror. I flinched as I took in the image—my hair was a wild knot of frizz, the corners of my mouth drooped down, tired. Dried sweat had left me wrinkled and salty.

Somehow I was convinced that if I could get inside that tank, some of that would change. Instantly.

Just in those few minutes at Mermaid Park, I'd caught a glimpse of something I didn't even know human beings could do. It was the most beautiful thing I'd ever seen.

The taxi driver took me all the way back to the motel, turning off the meter when the fare hit eight dollars, all I had in my pockets, which left him with no tip. Curiosity kept his eyes on the rearview mirror, on this girl, a 2 a.m. mystery on a dark road outside the place where mermaids really did exist.

In the courtyard, I saw Lynne, who had brought her small dog out to pee. When she saw me, she glanced at her wrist. She was wearing no watch.

"Just out for a stroll?"

"I got lost," I said. The most successful lies were always ones uncluttered by explanation. A nod toward upstairs. "Anybody miss me?"

She shrugged and shook her head no, watching her dog as he chewed on a dandelion stem. She said to him, "You probably shouldn't be eating that," but didn't make him stop. Then back to me, "So you guys go home tomorrow night. What are you doing with the rest of the summer?"

I had been choosing to not think about that—the long, endless days stretching out in front of me. What would I do? I would hide in my room and watch TV and sleep or go to Rebecca's and watch TV and sleep. It would make the time go faster till I went back for my next-to-last year of high school. Only two years left till I could move out and go to college, assuming I could get a partial scholarship for swimming.

But I only said, "I have no idea."

"Do you have a job?"

"No," I said. "That would require a car."

"Ah," she said. "All the kids down here get jobs. It's easier, I guess. You can walk everywhere."

I had a glimpse of myself walking to the boardwalk, where I would serve steaming slices of pizza to kids with painted faces, boys traveling in packs.

Maybe after work I could meet the guy from the pool, and we could follow our dark footsteps on the nighttime beach and see where it took us.

I knew Tom would never let me have something great like

that, but someday I'd be out of his house and he'd have no say. So I said, "Maybe my first summer in college, I could come down here and work somewhere."

Lynne smiled. "That would be nice," she said, seeming to mean it.

"Okay, thanks." I bent to pet her dog's silky-smooth fur, its curls giving off the scent of what I thought might be Pantene. Lynne bent and scooped him up and with the other arm caught me in a quick squeeze before she went back to her apartment.

Fatigue started to creep over me, but first, I was so thirsty my tongue stuck to the roof of my mouth. I went to the vending machines to get a soda, then felt my empty pockets. The cab ride—I'd forgotten. I rested my head against the cool machine and willed a can of anything to drop out.

"Are you okay?"

I jumped, then looked down to hide my smile as I saw that it was the guy from the pool. "Yes, just praying for a soda to appear." I tried to make my breathing normal, which was hard because it wanted to be fast.

He unzipped the pocket of his swim trunks, which were slung low on his hips. Flat abs peeked just over the top deliciously. My tired eyes stayed there, unable to look away, till I heard the sound of coins being slid into the machine.

I snapped awake when he said, "What kind did you say?"

"Are you my fairy godmother?" I asked, doing a good job of keeping my smile hidden. My heart was pounding like it wanted to escape from my chest.

"Some guys might take that as an insult," he said. "You know—the whole fairy thing. It doesn't bother me, but you know how guys can be."

"You're much too macho and self-aware for that."

"You read me well." His eyes were locked on mine, intense.

"Thanks. I try."

"Let's see how well I read you." He turned and faced the machine, started by pointing at the first push button. "Coke is too basic for somebody so complex."

I smiled. "Interesting. My soda horoscope. Keep going."

"Then we have Sprite," he said, turning to look at me. I saw that sunburn had pinked the tip of his nose, the apples of his cheeks. "But that's lemon-lime, which says sour, and you're sweet."

"Oh," I said, laughing now. "You are *smooth.*"

He smiled too and quickly glanced at my lips. Then, decisively, "Root beer is my pick for you." He pushed the button. A can clattered down into the tray.

"Why?"

"It's unusual. It looks like Coke in the glass, but when you taste it—it surprises you." He blew off the top of the can before he popped it open and handed it to me.

I raised it to my lips and drank. My throat burned as I gulped too fast. "So are you staying here?" I finally said.

"No." He gestured toward Lynne's office. "I work here sometimes, fixing things, taking care of the pool. Rescuing people."

I laughed, remembering my scabby chin, which pulled as I

smiled. "Well, I'm just visiting. Lynne is my mom's godmother," I said. "Her *real* godmother, not just a fairy one. She let us come down and stay."

"Lynne's goddaughter's daughter." He put it together out loud.

"Amy," I said back.

"Amy." He said it like he would remember it. "I'm Dylan. We've never met before?"

Smile. A shake of my head.

"It feels like I know you," he said quietly. Then, "You've been to Wildwood before?" Was that surprise in his voice, like he would've noticed me before if I'd been here? Or was that just what I wanted him to mean?

"Nope, first time here," I said. "My mom came down to Wildwood all the time growing up—that's how her family met Lynne and her family. I guess she burnt out on it or something. We usually go to Sea Isle or Atlantic City a couple of times every summer."

"Yeah, Sea Isle is okay," he said, not meaning it.

"Yeah, Wildwood is okay too," I said.

"I'm a little biased," he said. He pressed his lips together, like he was thinking about what it felt like when lips pressed against each other. I did the same thing without even meaning to.

"So I guess we've never met," I said. "Unless you come up to the city and save people there too?"

He shook his head. "I wish." His eyes went to the cut on my chin. A darker blue shifted in his eyes. I had a feeling I could watch those eyes for days and still not have seen all the colors. "I've been meaning to ask," he said, lowering his voice. "How long are you staying?"

"We leave tomorrow night." It sounded so soon, and I wanted to hear him be disappointed that I would be leaving so fast.

"Tomorrow night? You just got here."

I bit my bottom lip to keep from smiling. The tone, disappointment was there. I was torn—should I feel elated or gypped?

"That's my luck," I said.

"No, actually, that's *my* luck," he said.

"Are you really going to fight me over whose bad luck this is?" My voice was singsongy, sarcasm just under the surface.

He smiled. "Does that surprise you?"

I laughed. At every turn, there was a challenge with this guy. He moved to stand in front of me, the toes of our flip-flops touching. He was so close, I felt my spine straighten, shoulders pull back—the way I always meant to stand but never actually did.

I breathed into my hand to see if I had root beer breath, which was at least better than bad breath. I wondered quickly if Lynne would mind me getting kissed in her vending machine room.

With my hand at my mouth, my fingertips felt the salty-crusty residue of sand, dried sweat. Oh God. I suddenly remembered the reflection I'd seen in the mermaid tank—how scary I'd looked. I tried to remember if I'd put on mascara earlier, unsure if that too was melted down my face. Maybe Dylan hadn't gotten a good look, all the way across the dim room, red lit from the

Coke machine. But he was much closer now. Right there in front of me.

I definitely didn't want him seeing me now.

Still looking down at our flip-flops, I said, "Nice shoes."

"Thanks." He laughed, his breath warm in my hair.

"So," I said.

He paused, then said, "Tomorrow?"

"Tomorrow," I said, feeling a rush of relief.

He laughed again. "You're definitely a root beer," he said into the top of my head.

I slipped in the door noiselessly, hidden by the din of the AC. After dry-brushing my teeth in the dark and sleeking on a fresh coating of aloe lotion to take the sunburn sting away, I was stuck again in the middle spot between Mel and Trina. The aloe took on a Krazy Glue quality—with each gentle shift in their weight came a sharp, de-sticking pull, enough to keep sleep away.

Plus Mel was grinding her teeth viciously in her sleep. Half of me wanted to poke her awake and the other half had to stop in pure wonder—what in the world was she dreaming of? Was it the idea that a guy like Dylan could have picked me over her?

Dreamy, I felt sleep drifting nearby, just out of my reach.

Watery light, reflected from the pool, shifted and stirred in the room. I watched it, my mind back at that mermaid place, where I felt like I could float forever on shifting blue waters of a hundred different shades. I could almost smell the air rich with cut grass, nestled down in a safe nook of the earth. Around me fat crickets sang and sang, happy.

In that aquarium at the mermaid park and downstairs tonight, I had caught little glimpses of what could save me from me, and from all of this.

CHAPTER *Five*

IN THE MORNING, I FAKED BEING ASLEEP UNTIL EVERYONE LEFT FOR the beach.

It wasn't uncommon. Sleepless nights made me eerily unwakeable, and that's how I pretended to be when the rest of them headed to the beach, waiting until the afternoon to get up so I could take advantage of the last day here. I had different plans for myself.

Mom's note, written on a Noah's Bagels napkin in perfect Palmer-method cursive handwriting, confirmed my deep sleep—*Couldn't wake you! Saved you a bagel (in fridge). Come down—same spot—or stay out of the sun today, you're so burned!*

I checked my reflection in the mirror over the dresser and saw that she was right—I was a pinkish red, not unpleasant, but easily pushed over the edge by another day out there. I leaned in to check my chin—yesterday's thin, shallow scratches were covered in hairline scabs that pulled tight when I smiled, and I resisted the urge to pick at them.

In the bathroom, I took a long shower, shaved my legs, washed my hair. Washed yesterday off me. Today was a new day, one that I'd hopefully be spending with Dylan. I took a big squirt of Trina's Anti-Frizz Serum and worked it through my hair, then dabbed on some lip gloss and a coat of waterproof mascara. Up close to the mirror, I checked myself out—the makeup looked natural, pretty.

The one thing I'd forgotten to pack was a magazine or a book, so I started digging through Mel's bag, looking for something to borrow. I felt a book deep in the back zipper compartment of her suitcase, grabbed it, scanned the cover, and groaned. Some *Chicken Soup for the Teenage Soul* knockoff—that was the only crap Mel read, but it would have to do. I un-wedged the bagel from its spot between the MGD and Fancy Cashews in the mini-bar fridge and headed out to the balcony.

It was already scorching hot—in the mid-nineties. I quickly scanned the courtyard for Dylan, but he was nowhere to be seen. Clusters of gnats hovered over the surface of the pool, swarming lazily. I took a bite of cold raisin bagel, my least favorite kind, and opened the book.

The pink highlighting covering the pages was what I noticed first.

I was surprised—it looked like Mel, who wasn't a big reader, had gone through this book a bunch of times. Some passages were marked with stars and exclamation points in her handwriting, in different-colored inks.

One story had a paper clip marking it. Page 174, "What Really

Matters." I rolled my eyes at the title—how Dr. Phil. That's where I started to read.

One of the bravest souls I ever knew was a fourteen-year-old leukemia patient named Jason.

Whoa. I sat up straight and looked around me. No one was there. All my senses were suddenly hyper-aware. The only sound I could hear was my heartbeat, loud in my ears. I kept reading, my mouth opening wide as I flipped the pages.

Everything was there.

How he loved going to school, even when he'd have to run to throw up in the bathroom, sick from chemo treatments.

How his classmates would send him postcards from their vacations so he could see a little bit of the world.

It was horrible. The whole story she'd told us all, it was a lie, stolen from someone *else's* life.

I planted my feet on the patio to stop the sense of free falling. My hands shook as I flipped pages to other stories, searching for more highlights.

Each one contained grains of her life's events for the last couple of years—the teacher from Japan who'd taught her class the lesson of patience through origami. A homeless guy who she'd started stashing her lunch money for. A petition she was gathering signatures for and another one about her summer camp for poor kids. Even the deaf-mute girl she'd met and befriended at the 7-Eleven—a takeoff on Helen freaking Keller, page 108.

Between pages, my eyes would quickly scan the courtyard;

I expected Mel to appear. I didn't know what to do when I saw her. Her cracks ran deeper than I had thought—this proved it.

Mel had told us all these stories for two years. Two whole years.

She had bought things for Jason, this kid who didn't exist. She had come home with origami swans and frogs—where had she learned to do that? I pictured her alone in the library, heaps of crumpled origami paper beside her, following instructions from a book.

The dedication to the whole charade, it scared me.

And I wanted to know, why? Why would she do this?

A shrink would say this was a call for help, or attention, or love.

Was she *that* desperate?

My lips pressed together in anger. Mel was the one of the two of us who had it easier. Tom was less harsh with her. Mom, more mom-like. Yet she wanted more.

So what was I supposed to do, knowing this now? Sure, I could tell Mom, but what would that accomplish? That would build more concern, a troubled look washing over Mom's face, which was worse because it was just a reminder that that same worry was never spent on me.

Tom might even take her on a trip to Dairy Queen to celebrate her deep psychosis.

So I closed the book and placed it right where I'd found it, in the back of her suitcase. As I zipped the compartment, I thought, *Goodbye, Jason, and the gnawing worry that kept me up at night.* And goodbye to Mel too, sort of.

Back out on the balcony, my brain on overdrive, I wished for any kind of sound, another guest, Dylan, anything to break the quiet. I picked the fat raisins free from my bagel and lined them up on the orange plastic armrest of my chair with plans to launch them one by one over the railing and into the bush below.

I lined up my fingers, one over each raisin like piano keys, and squashed one for each word: Why. Am. I. Always. So. Goddamn. Stupid.

But before I got to *stupid,* a hand reached in and grabbed the raisin. Dylan. My breath let out in a big sigh, and I felt a smile pulling at my cheeks. How everything could turn like that, just seeing him.

"No beach today?" he asked. As if I wasn't just waiting here for him. It was nice of him to give me that.

I looked up to see him, a dark silhouette outlined by the sun. "Nope," I said, trying to sound like it was just coming to me unrehearsed. "I'm a little too fried from yesterday."

I heard him laugh and loved it as he rolled the raisin between his thumb and middle finger. He was *nervous* to see me. "Yeah," he said, "I saw them walking down there earlier. Noticed you weren't along."

I crossed my arms and hugged my elbows tight. He had *noticed.*

My cheeks had turned redder, or at least they felt that way. "So do you have stuff to do today?" Hoping we could have the whole day together.

He paused, and for a second I thought, *I blew it, he thinks I'm trying to get rid of him.* But then he said, "Actually, I was hoping to run into you."

There. It was out. I laughed. "I was hoping that too."

His head dipped, chin touching his chest. Those clear blue eyes grabbed mine, and for a second I lost my breath. My toes curled around the chipped iron railing, and I made myself hold his gaze, my chin raising itself high, higher, as if attached to a string.

I noticed how his eyes squinted a little when he smiled, finally breaking his gaze. He gestured down the hall toward the stairs, then said, "Want to see something?" and before he was done speaking, I was already following.

The stairway was a shady narrow space that trapped delicious cool air. I breathed in deep—the smell so green, rich, out of place. I licked my lips when we paused at the top, close enough for me to smell cinnamon gum on his breath, ready for him to lean in and press his lips against mine. Wanting to feel that. I would hold his face to feel the stubble on his chin, prickly on my fingertips. Slide my hands across his broad shoulders, feeling the muscles shift under his shirt. My eyes half closed and waiting, I was surprised when he pushed through the door to reveal sunlight.

The roof. Of course. The roof.

His skin was cool as he took my hand. My fingers naturally curled into the spaces between his, like they belonged there. I took another deep breath, smelling ocean and boardwalk and something else that was probably roof tar. I couldn't stop looking at him, me smiling at him smiling, both of us kind of laughing and squinting at each other.

"Welcome to the roof," he said.

But it wasn't just a roof. A sky blue tarp made a nice sunshade over a loungy area. A padded deck chair sat on a big square of Astroturf marked with a faded Denny's logo. Another chair, which looked homemade. An overturned bucket sat at footstool height.

"This is awesome," I said, wanting to touch all his stuff at once. I stood on the Astroturf, feeling the prickle of the plastic grass under my feet. "Foot massage," I said, taking stupid little steps around the rug. I held out my hand to him. "Come on— try it."

He laughed and kicked off his flip-flops, stepping onto the rug like I had. "Ohhhhh, yeah," he said, stopping and scrunching his toes. "Why do we ever wear shoes?"

"You just gave me an idea," I said, inching over to stand near him without looking right at him, suddenly a little shy. My voice softened. "No more shoes. Never again."

His arm brushed against mine a little. Lower, he said, "We'll burn all our shoes." The sun was so bright, he squinted at me through one eye.

"That might take a while. I have lots of shoes."

"I have lots of time."

I slid my hair over one shoulder and shaded my eyes to look at him. He bit his lip, nervous, those eyes meeting mine.

"So this is cool up here," I said, brushing back against his arm. I traced the *D* in *Denny's* with my toe. "Did you do all this?"

"A lot of this stuff I found on the beach," he said, taking off his backpack and sitting on the fake grass. I sat on the bucket, facing him. "This"—pointing up—"is a parachute, I think." I looked up, reached out, and touched it, nodding at its softness. Then, pointing at the chair, "I found one piece of the surfboard after a storm this winter, and the other piece washed up three months later," he said. "But look—they match." Amazingly, yes, they did. The pieces had found each other after three months apart at sea. "The best part, though, is the view."

I looked up and had to draw in a huge breath. How had I missed it?

Five blocks from the beach, you wouldn't expect it—a clear, wide-open, unobstructed view of sand, dotted with blankets, then the endless ocean. I scanned the beach for Mom and Tom, but from up here, the people looked so small, I couldn't tell—they could *all* be Tom for what I could see. On this clear day, I knew it was white hot, merciless out there. But here under the ice blue shade, with the soft slap-slap sound of the parachute, the day felt so different to me—I was dizzy with the sensations as the wind, which was cool up here, played with my hair.

I moved over to the surfboard chair, and he sat in the other one. For a while, we just stared out at the water, and I closed my eyes, trying to bring my breathing back to normal—I could feel my stomach tense with nerves, maybe with wanting to kiss him. Or more so, wanting *him* to kiss *me*. I peeked through my eyelashes to watch as he took in my face, my hurt chin, slowly working down my shirt while I barely breathed. His eyes reached my legs. "What happened?" I opened my eyes with a questioning gaze. "Your knee." I leaned up to look and saw that my knee had long, thin scratches radiating outward from it in a circle.

"I got pushed," I said. "I was looking at a horseshoe crab that had washed up on the beach last night, and Trina, my sister's friend, pushed me so I fell on it."

"Why would she do that?"

"That's just how she is," I said. Then, thinking about the book, "That's how they both are."

"Just born mean like that," he said.

"Yep."

"So what did you do?"

A sharp laugh came out. My eyes suddenly felt wet. "I walked off."

"Walked?" He sounded like he saw right through me.

My cheeks reddened. "Okay, stormed."

His head shifted to one side, figuring something out. "So that's where you were coming from last night."

I thought about the mermaid park, wondering if he knew

about it. But already I felt a little stupid, so I just nodded. "Thanks for the soda, in case I didn't say."

He reached out to tuck back a strand of my hair, and I pressed my lips together to hide the smile I felt. He saw it anyway.

"So, tonight." Just like that. My heart sped up, hearing the disappointment in his voice.

"It sucks," I said.

"Will you be back down this summer?" His light touch was on my knee, tracing the little scratches. It gave me goose bumps.

I thought of Tom, hanging around the house all day now that he was out of work, listening to sports radio.

"No," I said. "This is it. Until next summer, or college anyway. I might come down here to work one summer."

"Oh, yeah?" A bright tone, interested. I smiled. He smiled back.

"Light-years from now."

He slid an arm around my shoulders, and I nudged my chair closer, smelling his soapy cleanness, feeling the warmth of his arm around me. I took a big breath, hating the idea of over two months in front of a TV, avoiding Tom, when I could be here.

Out on the beach, I suddenly realized a steady trail of people had started making the trek back to the boardwalk, back toward home. I knew Tom and Mom and the girls would be among them soon. "I guess I should go," I said. "They'll be back soon and I need to pack."

What I really wanted to do was stay here and have him grab

me in his arms and kiss me, then help me devise a plan—say, cut some fuel line that would prevent the station wagon from working or have Lynne adopt me so I could just live here with her. Something impulsive that would show he was as crazy with this as I felt.

When I stood up, the wind hit me with its full gust. It sent my hair streaming back, blew my shirt tight against my chest—it felt good. Above me, the parachute rolled like storm clouds.

I felt him watching me. I looked down at him and felt a jolt, seeing the way his eyes fell on me. He liked me, the way I'd wanted to be liked and the way I hadn't thought someone like him ever would. And while some people might say that right there that should be enough—having this moment as a souvenir in my pocket, something I could take out and hold between my palms whenever I wished—it wasn't enough for me.

I wanted to stay.

The courtyard had come back to life. A new family unloading bags from a car. An old lady eating gourmet french fries from a paper cone, sharing with seagulls too fat to fly far.

Lynne was in the office when I got there. "Hi," I said, not wanting to disturb her.

She looked up from the computer. "Hi there." She took her glasses off and said, "That's better. Now I can actually see you." She looked at the dog, still asleep in one of the red guest chairs. "Some guard dog you are."

I laughed and tried to sound casual. "You busy?"

Lynne heard something in my voice. "Never too busy. What's up?"

My chest heated, red splotches starting to blossom now that it was actually time to ask her. What would Lynne want with a guest for almost the whole summer? I was retreating fast.

"Is it about Dylan?" she asked. I could hear a little teasing in her voice.

"Not exactly," I said, which it wasn't, exactly.

"Okay," she said, waiting.

"It's about me. It's about me staying," I said quickly.

"You want to stay? Down here? This summer?" She put together phrases, me nodding in between each one. "This is okay with your mom?"

"Well," I said.

"You want me to ask for you."

I said the next part quietly so she could say no if she wanted to without feeling too bad. "Would you mind?"

"I'd love you to stay down here," she said. "I'll talk to her." Relief washed over me, and she saw it on my face. She laughed. "Now go. I'll catch her on the way up."

CHAPTER *Six*

UPSTAIRS BY MYSELF, I WAS FIDGETY WITH WAITING. THE LATE-afternoon sun was still hot, but the wind had kicked up more, stirring things up. The day was getting ready for trouble.

The room was stifling hot when I returned. I turned on the TV and blasted the AC on max. Standing in front of the pumping vent, my hands pressing against the windowpane, my hair streaming back from my face, I could see myself in a pane of glass, just like the night before.

This time I saw that there was a shine in my eyes.

What would happen if I just ran off now? Ran off to the mermaid place and lost myself in the crowd in the bleachers? Could I find somewhere to hide there? Was there any way on this earth the rest of my family could just go home and go on with the summer, with me unaccounted for like that?

Then I could spend every day like today. Up on the roof, with Dylan. And maybe next time in the stairwell, before he opened the door to let the sunlight in, I could take his hand away from the door-knob. Lean in and kiss his lips.

I couldn't help smiling at the idea.

And just at that moment, my family entered the courtyard. This would be my only chance.

Mel headed up the steps with concentration; I knew that look. She was tired and hot. A quick thought crossed my mind, and I glanced over at her suitcase. Would she be able to tell I'd been in her bag? That I knew about the book? No way. It was exactly as I'd found it. If she were to learn about it, it would be on *my* terms.

Back in the courtyard, Mom was holding hands with Tom, both of them drifting up the steps slowly behind the girls.

I was willing Lynne to pop her head out of the office door and grab Mom. The very last opportunity, it was down to a matter of minutes. My hands gripped the wooden windowsill as I stared at the office door, thinking, *Open open open open.* Trying to turn the office doorknob with my mind and make her appear.

So when her door *did* open right then, I was shocked—maybe my luck *was* changing. I saw both Mom and Tom turn as she must've called, and I was hoping, knowing my only chance would be if Lynne got Mom alone, without Tom. *Keep walking, Tom. Let her go.*

I think it was just at that moment that Tom, sweating and sandblasted from the beach, caught a glimpse of me in the window, my hair blowing in the air-conditioned goodness, which I had all to myself. He quickened his step up the stairs.

Mom. Yes, she lingered—and she let go of Tom's hand and took a step down to Lynne. I watched them start to chat, nodding, nodding, yes, that's good. Nodding was good. Nodding was *great*.

Then Lynne must have dropped her voice because Mom stepped closer and the nodding stopped. I wished I could hear what she was saying. I couldn't, but Mom's expression I could read like a familiar storybook—her eyes cut up to Tom, who was still making his way toward the room, and then to me in the window, rosy and cool. While I had her eyes, I willed her to say yes.

Our motel room door burst open, and I could half hear Mel dropping her bags, quickly changing the TV channel from whatever I'd had on, then saying, "Move it—let me get some air."

My eyes were still on Mom, who was shaking her head now at Lynne, saying no.

No? No.

Of course it was a no. All I ever heard from them was no.

Melissa pushed me, trying to get between me and the AC vent. I glanced at her and all I could see inside my head were all those pink highlights, crazy stripes and asterisks marking made-up friends, a whole faked life.

She had lived so many lies. For two whole years—a level of commitment I hadn't known she had.

Trina pried at my fingers on the windowsill, trying to get at the air. I held on tighter and bumped Mel away with my hip, sharply, an angry move that should have told her to quit it.

And I heard myself saying, low, "No. No. No."

Trina started really digging at my hand, prying my pinkie finger loose.

Mel grabbed my elbow, pulling on it with her whole body weight.

"No, no, no," getting louder.

Lynne had just grabbed my mom's hand and was talking to her again, nodding gently, still trying. My breath caught in my lungs, full, hopeful. That's when Mom just shrugged at Lynne—like, *I can't help you.* And I knew it was all over.

I was going back home.

I wanted to jump through the window at them and beg. Then they would know how serious I was. How badly I needed this.

Just then, Mel bent my finger back in one sharp move and Trina butterfly-pinched the back of my arm. Fast I swiped at them blindly, once, twice, missing widely but swinging so angrily, my hand blasted the window—hard.

Too hard.

Sharp snaps sounded. Like when you're about to fall through ice.

In the window, my panicked reflection split, then split again.

Then the window just crumbled. A thundering *whoosh* sounded as an avalanche of glass dumped outward onto the concrete balcony. Sharp shards of window popped as the pieces crashed into each other and broke again.

My hand was still out there in midair, where I'd hit the window, just frozen like that. I lowered it to my side, feeling my whole body shake from deep inside.

Tom was breathing right there over my shoulder, but for once, he didn't say a thing. I almost wished he would, just to break the silence.

From the corner of my eye, I saw Mel and Trina lower themselves onto the bed. When I looked right at them, they both glanced away and I spit out a laugh. "This is all *your* fault," I said.

Mel studied her hands in her lap. Tom moved to stand by her side and muttered something low and comforting that I couldn't quite make out. Outside, I heard Mom rushing up the steps. When she reached the door, Mom just looked at me. She said, "My God, Amy." Her voice was low and thick in the back of her throat. She looked scared. "I don't know what to do with you."

Her fear threw me. My knees went rubbery and loose. "Mom," I said softly.

"Don't," she said. Then a long pause. She looked at Mel and Trina on the edge of the bed. Tom had a hand on each of their shoulders.

Then the full weight of her gaze fell back on me. "I don't know where you get this," she said. "I don't know who you are when you act like this."

My knees wanted to bend and ease me down on the floor right there, even with the sharp cubes of glass glinting light at me, but I fought it. I couldn't look any of them in the eye, I was focusing so hard. Truth be told, I was probably more scared than any of them.

Tom broke the quiet by moving to the dresser and starting to pack, and one by one they all joined in. Trina crept behind me and bent out the window to pick up her hair-care bottles, stirring the glass cautiously. Hearing the tinkling of glass made me relive the window avalanche all over again, and that made my knees not want to hold me up.

Woozy, I reached my hands out, but there was nothing left to hold on to. With everyone's open suitcases covering the beds, I saw there was no room for me. So I made my way downstairs to find something to clean up the mess.

In the courtyard, I bumped into Lynne, who was headed upstairs with the same idea as me. I reached out to take the steel garbage can, dustpan, and broom, but she held on to them till I looked up.

Then she said, "I know that was an accident. Why didn't you say?"

I shrugged, still feeling the sting of Mom's last words. "They don't listen. They see what they want to see. Before it even happens sometimes."

"Are you okay?"

For the first time I looked down at my hand. The pad of my palm, right under the thumb, was sore and red, but no skin was broken. I held up my hand to show her. She took it and ran her own thumb over my skin to see, holding it up to the light for inspection. Eyebrows raised. "That was luck."

I almost laughed.

Behind me, I heard footfalls coming down the steps. Mom's

voice, from the darkness. "Amy, come over here. I need to talk to you."

Lynne retreated, and I walked over, still rubbing my palm.

After the silence stretched out, and I waited for her to start, looking down, frozen still, Mom sighed. "I don't get it," she said. "You could've really hurt somebody. Do you want to apologize?"

My head reared back in surprise, eyes angry. I was the one whose hand went through a window. Apologize? She saw my reaction before I could ice over again.

"God, everything we say or do just makes you mad," she said with bewilderment.

All I heard was the "we," which was meant to include her, Tom, and Mel, but not me. So I shrugged, defensive with sarcasm. "What can I say?"

Her head rolled back on her long neck, looking up to the sky. She was probably using that anger-countdown thing she'd learned in one of her nighttime community-college management courses—a trick to retaining composure. I could hear bones cracking; the long tendons in her neck made graceful hollows.

To the sky, she said, "You always have to make bad situations worse. All this hate, you've turned yourself into an angry person."

"*I've* turned myself?" I said with a biting laugh, daring her to meet my eyes.

She rolled her head down, lifted her eyes to mine. A shadow passed across her eyes. She let it go.

Too bad. I had thought we were getting somewhere.

Then she said, "I'm going to tell Lynne I want you to stay down here for the summer."

My breath caught in my throat. I glanced up to the rooftop, wondering if Dylan was up there. Fighting the urge to run up there and burst out onto the roof and shout to him: *I can stay!*

Then she said, "I think some time apart is what we need," finishing it.

The space I was breathing through felt like it was growing smaller and smaller. A rushing sound filled my ears. My heart beat loudly—I wondered, could she hear it too?

Raisin bagel churned in my stomach. For a second, I thought I might throw up.

Mom was already walking toward the office, leaving me alone at the poolside, not even waiting for me to respond or say okay.

This had been *decided*. Without me.

"You'll need to work to pay for the window to get fixed, too," she called to me over her shoulder as she opened the door. "Probably two hundred dollars. Maybe more." She closed the door behind her, the slam sounding louder than it should have.

This wasn't how I'd wanted it.

I felt heavy, was having trouble standing up on my legs.

So I sat on the edge of the pool, down at the deep end. Stuck my feet in the warm water. The blue pool lamp was right there under me, and it cast giant shadows of my feet over the entire pool bottom.

They were so much bigger than I felt.

CHAPTER *Seven*

WATCHING THEM LEAVE WAS WEIRD. TRINA WAS HYPER-ALERT FOR once, coming downstairs with her duffel bag stuffed, trying to figure out the dynamic of what was going on. Her dark eyes slid from face to face; somehow she knew better than to ask.

"So," Melissa said, walking up and standing near the edge of the pool. Blue light underlit her small, pretty features. I was hit by a hint of worry—this crazy girl, alone with Tom for the next couple of months—a position I surely wouldn't have wanted to be in.

She cast a furtive glance over her shoulder to make sure we were alone. Then she looked me right in the eye. I saw how her eyes were sharper suddenly, the skin around them tight with jealousy. She said, "You're always such an asshole, and now it pays off."

Oh. Like this.

I couldn't leave her feeling superior for the entire summer. I wanted her to be sunk low, like me.

So I leaned in close, and I said to her softly, "I know."

She let out a sharp laugh, not getting it. "You *know* you're an asshole?"

I leaned closer and whispered, "No, Mel. I know. About the book."

I could see her confusion; then suspicion drew her brows down low over her tight gaze. "What book?"

Her acting skills faltered just a little right then. Color drained from her face. Her teeth clenched to keep her jaw from shaking. I saw it all, and so I said coolly, "Do you *have* more than one book?"

"You don't know anything," she said. Hatred made her eyes shine.

She wanted more, but Tom had descended to the courtyard. Mom had pulled him out to the balcony to tell him I was staying. I heard them exchanging hushed words—he was unhappy about me staying. He'd rather I spent the summer filling potholes with the community improvement volunteers or just holed up in my room at home, with nothing to do but wonder what he might do next.

But as it turned out, when you shared one motel room with four people, there wasn't room for debate.

So that was how I stayed.

He spun his car keys on his middle finger, his volume turned up to high, retaking control of the situation. "Train is leaving! I repeat, the train is leaving!" He liked it this way, leaving late at night when the highways were open wide. Sleepy drivers sharing his roadway were always startled by his driving, unnecessarily aggressive on what were pretty much open roads.

Mom came up next to me and waited for me to get up. Lynne, nearby, looked at me, then looked away, uncomfortable with the standoff. I stayed seated. Mom squatted down on her heels with a sigh and cocked her head, studying my face. I waited for her to say something, maybe to apologize, my eyes watching the water, on the drain twelve feet down, lower than my heart would let me go, where debris danced in the suction.

But after a bit, she just stood up and I heard the sound of shoes turning on concrete, and they all left together, just like that.

I hadn't said a thing. Mostly out of embarrassment. If I'd opened my mouth, I would have let out one of those howling cries you see on the Discovery Channel. Every motel room's door would have cracked open, people peering out, nosy to see who was hurting.

Off a little in the distance, I heard the tinkling of glass being swept up and dropped into the trash.

Twelve hours later, waking up on Lynne's sofa bed, I felt weird. In my head, I ticked through all the normal weirds I knew. No, this wasn't out-of-place weird, or they're-talking-about-me weird, or even sick weird.

I finally put my finger on it. Excitement. About the unknown, and being here in Wildwood with a whole day stretching out in front of me like a green pasture.

This place, this town, was worth getting out of bed for.

Mermaids really existed here, and surely that meant I could do magical things here too. Granted, soon I would need to get a job, but the promise of a couple days of pure vacation by myself was enough to make me smile with delight.

Late-morning sun streamed in the big open window over the sofa. I looked at the clock on the cable box—ten-thirty. Outside, kids played, splashing water and laughing. I was awash in the possibilities of it all and wondering if Dylan knew yet that I was here. After I'd quickly made the bed and folded it away, I saw that Lynne had Mom's high school graduation picture in a frame on the wall. I knew it was Mom—her tiny chin, like a doll's. The delicate necklace she still wore sometimes—a slim gold chain with three tiny pearls in a row; I used to count them, one two three, when I was little and sitting in her lap. Under the picture, I noticed Lynne's miniature shelf of doll china over the sofa—cups small enough to fit over the tip of my pinkie, painted with pink tea roses. I picked one up and placed it in the center of my palm to get a closer look, struck by a feeling of my own giantness. As I glanced around, I realized for the first time that Lynne seemed to have a real fascination with small things.

On the coffee table, a dish of mints from Italy, each the size of a pencil eraser, wrapped in its own little piece of silver foil.

Travel-size soaps, mini-shampoos, toothpastes in the bathroom in a big basket under the sink—all different kinds, and I had my pick. Charmed, I spent five minutes choosing. Lynne's washcloths were embroidered with the smallest seashells you'd ever see—conch, scallop, conch, scallop, kindly taking turns all around the border.

I took my time shaving my legs, knowing I might see Dylan. Maybe we could go down to the beach together. Lie down on a towel next to each other so we could be close-close. Our sandy feet entwined, playing with the scratchiness. His arm stretched out under my head, his bicep a nice pillow. Or maybe we could get together with some of his friends, and if they had girlfriends, well, they were welcome to come too. We could just hang out somewhere. Maybe the roof? I could sit on Dylan's lap on the chair—the one made of two surfboard pieces that had found each other after being torn apart at sea.

After a long shower, I slipped on my swimsuit and a pair of loose khaki shorts, sky blue flip-flops. I took a couple of magazines from the office area and headed out to the pool. I pulled a lounge chair to the shady corner, where I could see the billowing of Dylan's parachute-tarp if the wind blew just right.

The heat had mercifully broken overnight. Today the air was a mild eighty-five. The humidity was all gone; a few plump white clouds broke up the wide expanse of sky. I debated between *Marie Claire* and *Lucky* and chose *Lucky* because it had a better name—plus a cover line promised "We road-test tooth whiteners." I flipped pages and read, listening to the Best of the Eighties Memorial Day Countdown on somebody's radio, tapping my toes and looking at pictures of hundred-dollar shoes that I hoped I would one day be able to buy by the dozen.

The combination of the sun and the breeze started to make me sleepy. And soon I was in a flawless hotel lobby in Paris, where nobody knew me, and I was buying perfect thimble-sized replicas of the Eiffel Tower and the Louvre to bring back as proof of my journey.

Oui, *I am here by myself,* I said to admirers three deep surrounding me. *Me? Brave? Independent? Oh, go on. Would you like some more baguette and Brie? Du vin? Can I direct you to the post office, by chance?* I caught a reflection in a hotel door and saw that I wasn't in the right body. The face looking back at me was completely foreign, a stranger, and I didn't know where the real me had gone off to or how I'd gotten to where I was and if I should even be worried about all that.

The sound of Lynne's voice brought me back. She was directing two workmen who were carrying a heavy pane of glass into the courtyard—they were headed upstairs to replace the window I'd broken. They navigated the steps expertly, and watching them, I was momentarily blinded by the hot glare of the sun reflecting off the glass.

Suddenly self-conscious, I sat up abruptly and straightened my stack of magazines.

The clock over the office door said two-thirty—I had slept away most of the day, and Dylan hadn't even come around. I pushed away the disappointment and reminded myself that if this summer was going to be different, it was time for me to stop waiting around and start looking for a job. I headed inside to change.

The first help-wanted sign I spotted was in the window of a jewelry shop on the boardwalk. Inside, I was overcome by the scent of incense and music heavy with African drumbeats. I tried to look engrossed in a display case, waiting to be approached.

I could work in a place like this.

Velvet pads filled with gold necklaces and charms broadcasting the owner as #1 Daughter or Dad or Nana or Grad. "That one is great on you," I would say sincerely.

A figure to my left suddenly shifted. Oh, a person. A middle-aged woman with hair down to her waist; she'd been sitting there the whole time. "You want to see the pipe?" she asked with flat directness.

I looked down to see what she meant. Oh. The counter I'd been staring into this whole time was filled with what looked like bongs, pipes—stuff to smoke pot with. I had been so caught up in my head, I hadn't even noticed.

"No!" I blurted, too loud. Then, not wanting to seem like it offended me, "I mean, no, thanks." She settled back on her stool.

As I moved on to the next counter, I tried to picture myself selling one of the shiny, fake-jewel-encrusted pipes to a customer. "Now this one," I'd say, holding up the mirror. "I think this one really, truly suits you." My head would nod a little too enthusiastically, trying to make up for the fact that I'd never even smoked pot and had no idea how to load a pipe or even if *load* was the right word.

"You change your mind about that pipe, I'll give you a good deal," she said. Her belly, exposed under her short top, was fleshy and folded. "Best deal on the boardwalk."

"Oh, that's good to know," I said, wondering if she couldn't tell I was sixteen or if she just didn't care. I merged with the crowd and fled, thinking how I couldn't have worked in that much incense anyway since it gave me headaches.

Farther north on the boardwalk, I was lured into one of those restaurants that served oversized pizza slices; you'd have to fold them in half to eat them, while a trail of grease worked its way down to the tip of your elbow. Inside was a massive dining room swarming with families, happy children sticky with grape drink.

Behind the counter, older Italian men yelled out to the crowd, "Hot slice!" "Come and get it!" And to girls in bikinis, "I got your hot slice, honey," overly lewd, so it made everybody laugh. The restaurant was busy and alive.

A place like this, it was friendly, in constant motion. I could make great money here. Maybe some friends, too.

A woman at the cash register barely glanced at me as she punched in numbers and slid a credit card. "You need something?"

I said, "Are you guys hiring?"

Rather than answering, another fast glance. Swipe-swipe with another card; her long nails were decorated with rhinestones. "Experience?"

"Oh, yeah," I said, gesturing big with my hands. "Experience." Granted, never waitressing, but other things, sure, I had experience.

"Wait over there," she said, waving toward a corner booth.

The booth was filled with all the waitresses' purses, jackets. A burning cigarette smoldered in the black plastic ashtray. A waitress had a whole line of ketchup bottles resting mouth to mouth, merging their contents. She looked bored. A couple of booths away, preteen boys glanced longingly from their baskets of fries to her ketchup bottles.

"Do you make good tips here?" I asked the waitress.

"That was my last tip." She pointed at a wet puddle of pennies surrounded by ketchup lids. "And I had to fish it out of the bottom of some asshole's lemonade cup."

Okay, so I'd landed the one unfriendly waitress. I looked around the room, surveying the crowd. I made a game of trying to gauge tipping potential. The three ketchup-less boys—maybe fifty cents. A young family with three sand-covered kids—the littlest one stuck on the back of the booth, trying to climb over into the next table, parents too tired to reprimand him—they were good for maybe a buck. Similar customers dotted the other tables. My head sank lower on my shoulders, counting up the odds. Reading one unfriendly face after another.

An older man was talking to the cashier, probably the owner.

Soon she would tell him about me, and there would be no escape. I felt the seconds ticking on my last chance to bail. From behind the pizza counter, I heard deep-voiced shouts of, "I got your slice, bay-bee!" One of the waitresses emerged from the kitchen laughing, with man-sized flour handprints on her butt.

I stood up abruptly, knocking the table a little in my rush. The ketchup bottles swayed like drunks.

"Whoooa," the waitress said, her arms outstretched in a semicircle in case any fell, which they didn't. "You're lucky," she said to me.

"Yeah," I said as I headed to the door, "I keep hearing that."

A long line snaked through Burger King, like for one of the boardwalk rides, but instead of a roller coaster, you'd get a Happy Meal. Or wait, that was McDonald's—what was Burger King's kids' meal called? I stood off to one side of the counter, waiting for one of the cashiers to look my way so I could ask for an application. Finally I walked up to the skinny cashier, who said without looking up, "Welcome to Burger King, can I take your order?"

The sun visor hid his eyes; all I could see was angry red acne on his cheeks. I said, "I'd like an application, please."

He held his finger poised over the touch-screen menu, going down each column of buttons—FRIES, ONION RINGS, WHOPPER JR. W/CHEESE—looking for the button that said APPLICATION. I waited for him to realize, shifting my weight from foot to foot, feeling the line loom large behind me. "No food," I finally said, embarrassed, "just an application for a job. "

He reached under the counter and handed me a form. I took it to a sticky table and fished a pen out of my bag.

Name, easy. Address, that was trickier—did they want home or Lynne's? I wrote down Lynne's but didn't know the zip code, so I left that blank. Social security number? I couldn't remember the last few digits of mine; left it empty. Lynne's phone number? No clue. I put in the area code—609—then just made up seven digits.

I went back and made up a social security number too.

I got creative in "work history." I wrote down a restaurant near my mom's office, and under that I wrote *cook's assistant*. This was getting fun. I filled in the rest of the lines—housekeeper for Tom's, Inc., and *general office duties* because I'd spent a couple of sessions in the principal's office in the last year, and I thought that should count toward something.

The manager had the ear-to-ear smile of someone fresh from a customer-service seminar at corporate. A jumbo button on her red-and-orange-striped shirt said, I'M SHAWNA. HOW CAN I HELP YOU TODAY? She glanced at my paper and said, "You have a lot of experience for a sixteen-year-old."

"I started early," I said.

"Okay, I'll check references and give you a call."

I held steady. "Check references?"

"Procedure," she said. Pointing to the 609-something number I'd made up. "Is this where I can reach you?"

"Sure," I said.

I burst out the door, hot-faced and smelling like french fries. This sucked. I needed a job—I had to pay for that stupid window. But all I could think of was how I needed another shower or a cool bath.

Or a dip in a deliciously blue pool.

A small shiver passed through me. And I knew some little part of my mind had been bringing me north all this time on purpose. Not too far off in the distance, when I looked at the ocean, I could see the familiar outline of the lighthouse and the spot where the jetty broke the wide expanse of sand—foamy waves crashed over the black rocks, making the waters calm as they rolled onto the sands of North Wildwood.

The mermaid place. Of course. I turned and headed that way, my pace quicker than before.

CHAPTER *Eight*

TIRE TRACKS MARKED THE DUSTY ROAD LEADING BACK TO THE mermaid park. A cool pocket of air hung here—the treetops kept the day's sun at bay, creating a feeling of being indoors for the people underneath.

The parking lot was mostly empty. A few minivans, station wagons, one even wood-paneled like Tom's. Not his, though—I could tell by the bumper sticker, which read, I BRAKE FOR YARD SALES. I knew firsthand that Tom slowed down as he passed yard sales, but only so he could open his window to yell, "Crap for s-a-a-a-ale! Please buy my crap!" My shoulders hunched just thinking about it.

The fact was, I knew I was procrastinating, killing time as I stood out in the green-scented air. After a morning of dead ends, I was a little worried, and maybe a little superstitious, too. Because this was where I really belonged this summer—not selling bongs to people who reeked of incense and something else, something more pungent. Not fishing tips out of the bottom of lemonade cups, wiping flour handprints off my ass. But what if they didn't want me?

I was scared because I could feel the rightness of this place seeping into my pores. In the cool, wet air, my hair clumping into spirals like it did whenever I was somewhere damp.

This place, it just felt good to be here.

I didn't care what I'd have to do—pick kids' gum off the bottom of bleachers, sell tickets, whatever. I just wanted to work at the park.

While Mel was at home in her room with her pink highlighter poised over someone else's sad story, I would be spending my days with the mermaids. And every night, I could go home to the motel and see Dylan. It was everything I ever could have wanted—right there in my lap, not even twenty-four hours after my family had taken off without me.

And that's what scared me into standing still—when I wanted something this badly, it usually got messed up. I would end up empty-handed and angry.

It had happened when I'd pushed to get my license, which, thanks to a badly mangled traffic cone, now I couldn't get till I was seventeen. It had happened too many times to count.

But then it hit me—it hadn't happened this summer. Here I was, still down at the shore. Maybe it hadn't happened how I would have wanted, but it had happened anyway.

That right there—that broke the losing streak. Or at least gave me a glimpse of what could be; that there were more answers than no. I felt myself lifting my shoulders, my chin. I set my eyes on the turnstile, the gate to where I was going and where I wasn't leaving without a job.

The girl behind the counter was a couple of years older than me and slender, fair, and red-haired—the look that told you that in another life she might've actually been a mermaid. As if to prove otherwise, she had her long white legs and bare feet perched on the aged wood counter while she watched a small black-and-white TV whose antenna jutted out into the walkway. Wrapped around her big toe was a Smurf Band-Aid.

"Hey," I said.

"Admission is seven bucks," she said absently, not looking up from the screen.

"Oh, actually, I wanted to talk to somebody about working here."

She barely glanced up, one slender shoulder rising in a half shrug. "We're not hiring."

"Well, maybe I can talk to the manager or somebody," I said. Just beyond the turnstile, I could hear the music starting over the tinny speakers. "You know, just to be sure."

She let out a sarcastic laugh. "I *am* sure. Bruce only hires from the waiting list—there are tryouts every spring. You can put your name on the list, but that means a job next summer *if* you're even qualified."

Had I been totally wrong about this place?

A little heat crept up into my cheeks, and I knocked down the urge to turn and go. Down below, the music started to swell louder. Fine, then—I could at least go in as a paying customer. I took a ten out of my pocket and slid it across the counter. "Hurry up—I don't want to miss the show."

This time I went closer, to the fifth or sixth row, behind all the families with little kids who were seated in the front. From this close, I could see the vastness of the tank—the rounded glass wall I faced must've been twenty-five, thirty feet tall. The very top of the tank was cleverly hidden from view—if there was a deck above for the mermaids to dive in, it was blocked from us in the audience by a high fence painted with sailboats, happy surfers, pelicans to make us think it was the ocean's surface.

No mermaids were inside the tank yet—just a backdrop painted with five-foot-tall seashells and long limbs of seaweed, all a little distorted through the glass. From inside, the audience must have looked odd and stretched, like people come alive from a fun-house mirror.

When three mermaids shot into view from the *bottom* of the tank, the audience made a surprised, "Oh!" All thinking, *How could that be?* They swam swiftly, menacingly in a circle, each following another's tail, which kicked as though it were a single muscle clad in green-blue shimmer, letting us get used to the sight of them. Their dramatic black eyebrows, painted on, told us they were up to no good. But part of my head was somewhere else, having trouble getting around something—these girls, they were under about twenty-five feet of water right then. I knew that the strong, powerful strokes they were using took a lot of air. Yet none of them were headed for the surface.

Tiny air bubbles trickled up through the tank's clear water, like in champagne.

I knew it was impossible, but somehow these mermaids were *breathing underwater.*

Quickly the mermaids scattered, hiding behind shells and plastic seaweed as a new backdrop floated up from below—a sea castle, a bigger version of the kind you'd put at the bottom of your aquarium. We watched them swim into the castle door and disappear, then reappear in an upstairs window, their bedroom, brushing their long blond hair with combs made of pearls, applying red lipstick from a golden tube, the song lyrics explaining that the princesses were getting ready for the ball, where they would try to win the heart and the riches of the prince. Little girls in the front row giggled and played with their hair, pretending to get ready too. It came to me then, this story, why it felt familiar—it was the underwater version of *Cinderella.*

When the castle descended and a new backdrop slid in, we met her in a small kitchen, the poor and hardworking girl who I knew would, in the end, fit the glass slipper, or the glass flipper, or whatever thing they decided to substitute for a shoe in this story without human feet. The plot didn't matter as much to me anyway as the swimming—with her legs bound together, her long, dark hair tied back with a tattered rag, this new mermaid had a calm, powerful movement that was grace underwater.

The beauty of it had me spellbound. I wondered how I would look in there, how that would feel, knowing all these people sat breathless, watching me.

If Brian Hunter saw me in there, I knew he would remember me next time. Maybe even kick himself for blowing his chance with me. Regret his terrible misstep.

I realized it must be her—the same mermaid I'd seen here the other night. Could I do what she was doing? The strength of the swimming—that much I knew I had. What I could never pull off was the total gracefulness and excitement that had rendered us all in the audience motionless, even the little girls, who'd stopped their playing and now just stared undistracted.

At the end of it all, I stayed put while the knot of families and kids made their way up the bleachers, maybe to the gift shop or the exit. Walking up, the kids still craned their necks to see back into the tank, which seemed to be empty now except for a few cutout fish going back and forth, pulled on sticks by someone at the top of the tank.

A little girl said, "Mommy, that was a *real* mermaid. I could tell." The mom smiled at me, sharing the joke. I smiled back but thought, *I might be closer to the little girl on this one, lady.*

My heart was still pumping like crazy. This was how I felt during a swim meet or when I could feel Dylan watching me in *that* way—the excitement rushing through me, yet still comfortable in a place where I belonged. I could be part of all this, this thing that made my heart beat fast, inside a more perfect little universe than the one out there.

I waited in the back of the amphitheater as the crowd filtered out, looking for the right person to talk to. Way down in front, a sharp-faced older woman was collecting trash, bending slowly to pick up each piece. I went back and forth, deciding if I should talk to her. Then I saw a man coming down the ladder from a room overlooking the whole park—probably about sixty but moving quickly for a guy that age. I shot a glance at the equipment up there—a microphone, wires, light switches. Okay, I figured, maybe he was the maintenance guy or the technical expert. Before I could think too much, I followed him.

Quiet footsteps on the packed-dirt path. Standing close behind, him still unaware, I took him in—the broad shoulders that were strong but layered with extra heft. The damp air had left his undershirt wrinkled, and the start of sweat stains was already emerging under his arms. I willed him to turn from the box of cords he was sorting through, his breath heavy from the climb down the ladder, but he didn't. Finally I cleared my throat. "Sorry to bother you," I said.

He cast a short glance over his shoulder. If he was surprised by my approach, he didn't show it. "The show is over," he said.

"I know," I said. "I just saw it. It was wonderful."

He hadn't turned toward me, which would've been my invitation to continue. So I just kind of stopped. In his profile, his broad jaw, unshaven, was set and unsmiling. His eyes remained downcast. "What are you still here for?"

"A job." My hands had started to sweat, a lot, really. In my head, I tried to figure out what I'd do if he wanted to shake hands. I looked around quickly for somewhere to dry them.

His jaw clenched from impatience with me. "You can sign up on the list for next summer. Go up to the counter and the girl will give it to you."

"Well, thanks, but I need a job *this* summer."

"I don't have a job for you. We don't need anyone else."

I breathed out quietly but didn't budge. "You don't understand. I can swim."

A quick shake no. A quicker laugh. "You don't get it. There's more to it than swimming." He started to walk down the path that led to the audience seating and the mermaid tank.

That familiar red sting had come to my cheeks, and I hated it. A flash of Tom, his finger in my face, and my voice welled up high like a tide. "I mean it," I called after him seriously but holding in anger. "I can swim. I'm in the top two of my varsity team. My mom was once a state-ranked swimmer—I learned from her."

All I heard was a faint call back. "Tryouts will be next spring. That gate should be closed when you leave."

Screw next summer. I only had *this* summer.

I went through the turnstile and slammed the gate shut with a satisfying clink.

I walked down the boardwalk, staring at my feet, watching plank after plank disappear. The sun hung low in the sky, and seagulls cawed all around me.

Damn him. I knew I belonged there.

Beside me, I heard a light squeak of bike brakes. I moved aside to let the bike pass, but it didn't go past, just followed slowly. Finally I stopped with a huff and turned.

"Hi." It was Dylan.

His smile stretched wide, and I saw dimples I hadn't noticed before.

My breath caught with surprise, and I felt my smile taking over my face stupidly. I wanted to throw my arms around him and bury my face in that smooth spot in his neck, let my lips work their way up past his ear till finally they found his mouth. But instead, I just stood there.

"That's usually where you say hi back," he said. He brushed back a few hairs that hung in front of his eyes. His forearms were golden tan, nicely muscled.

"Hi back," I said, my head shaking it off, embarrassed.

"You stayed," he said. "Lynne told me earlier. I was hoping to find you, figured you might be on the boardwalk."

I smiled and took a big breath, trying to stand up a little straighter without obviously sticking my chest out at him. "I'm glad you found me," I said.

"What are you up to?"

"I was looking for a job," I said. The sting from the mermaid park ran fresh through me as I said the words.

"Any luck?"

I shrugged. "Not a good day," I said, even though right then, it was kind of starting to feel like a not-too-terrible day.

"Well, maybe I can change that," he said, sounding shy.

I realized I'd been holding my breath, so I took a big one.

"Can I offer you a lift?" he asked.

I laughed and looked at the mountain bike. "Is this where I ride on your shoulders?"

He drew his brows together, playing confused. Both grateful for the silly break in the tension. "You're kidding me," he said. "You've never ridden double?"

"I lead a sheltered life."

"C'mon," he said, sliding off the seat and straddling the T-bar. "You sit here." He patted the seat. I came closer; noticed he smelled like something spicy and wondered if he'd maybe put on cologne for me.

My heart quickened. "Then *you* climb on *my* shoulders?"

"Hop on," he said. "Then you can check off 'ride double on a mountain bike' from your list of things to do in life."

I felt him tense or flex a little as I touched his upper arm and climbed on, loving the shifting muscles. "Okay?"

"Now put your feet on the thingy sticking out of the back wheel."

"Is that the technical name for it?"

He laughed. Even in profile, his smile stole my breath. "Who's the expert here?"

I laughed too and steadied myself. "My feet are officially on the thingy."

"Then here we go," he said, setting one foot on a pedal. We

took off gently—him just riding standing up. I held on to the belt loops on his loose khaki shorts.

And every once in awhile, he'd look over his shoulder to see if I was okay. We'd lock eyes and smile, me squinting happily into the wind that rippled his T-shirt. It was the exact same color as his eyes and the sky that would stretch out over the rest of the summer, cloudless.

That's what made me decide for sure.

The next day, I'd be going back to that park. It was the last link missing, keeping this summer from being what I was dreaming of.

Tomorrow I would not leave that park without a job.

CHAPTER *Nine*

THE NEXT MORNING, I WAS THERE BEFORE THE PARK OPENED.

I'd barely slept, and when I had finally dozed off, I'd dreamt I was back at home in Philly, alone in our house. In my dream, water started seeping in through the living room carpet, rising quickly to my ankles, my knees, and as I tried to flee, I found that all the doors in the house were gone. All the windows were sealed. As the water rose to my shoulders and I began to float up to the ceiling, my tiptoes finally leaving contact with the carpet, I pressed my palms against the wet glass on the big living room window, certain I was going to die.

When I finally broke from the dream, I sat up on the sofa, waiting for my breathing to slow down, and put on the TV without volume. Infomercials and sitcom reruns kept me half awake for the remainder of the night. I flipped to a Mexican soap opera during a bedroom scene, and my sleepy eyes locked on the way the couple's hands touched each other's faces when they kissed. I wondered if Dylan and I would do that and decided I'd like to try.

The night before, when he'd dropped me off, there had been no kiss. Again. Now that there'd been so much buildup, it couldn't just be a passing smack—it would have to be bigger.

A little after sunrise, I left Lynne a note and took a long, slow walk north up the boardwalk to Mermaid Park.

The lot was empty when I arrived, the security fence locked. I parked myself on a mossy stump right outside the gate. The next person who crossed this threshold was going to be mine.

I had to wait nearly two hours. A hand-painted sign propped up at the ticket counter told me the first show started at ten, so I waited, and fifteen minutes before, a rusting Honda hustled into the lot and came to a quick halt in the closest parking spot. Two girls climbed out—I thought I recognized them from yesterday, but with sunglasses and without the heavy makeup, I wasn't so sure. It was a little jarring somehow, the contrast of the image of beautiful mermaids burned into my mind and these girls who looked so . . . regular. They started unloading bags from the trunk just as two minivans pulled into the lot, crackling gravel and leaving trails of dust.

"Shit, shit, shit," one girl said, starting to grab at the bags more quickly.

The darker girl, whose hair fell in a smooth curtain to hide half her face, said, "Just hurry."

The other girl threw a duffel bag strap over her shoulder, and in her haste a bundle of makeup pencils and tubes dumped and scattered across the gravel lot. She gasped and glanced at the vans, just starting to unload with kids. "Shit, they're going to see us with legs. Bruce will have a fit."

I knew a chance when I saw one, so I darted over to their car. "Go ahead, get inside," I said. "I'll bring this stuff back to you." I knew I sounded certain and firm, already using both hands to pick up eyeliner, lip liner, a tube of waterproof blush cream that smelled like freesia.

The blond girl slid her sunglasses up to her forehead and squinted at me, trying to figure out who I was. After slamming the trunk closed, the second girl paused and looked at me too.

My hands started to sweat as they filled with pencils and tubes.

Crap. They weren't leaving.

This wasn't going to work. I was never going to get inside.

Just then, the sound of another car pulling into the lot was like sweet music to my ears. Like a gunshot, it cut short any questions the girls might've had. I heard their feet beat quick steps toward the gate.

My hands gripped the makeup pencils so hard they might've snapped. Blood pumping so fast, I swear I could just about hear it whooshing in my ears. As I got to the foot of the bleachers, the mermaid tank loomed giant over me, like the sheer face of a tidal wave.

It was huge and deeper than I'd thought on my last visit.

Pressing my cheek against the cold glass, I tried to peer all the way to the top—which was tricky because the glass was a few inches thick and coated with the thinnest carpet of bubbles inside, which caught the light and played tricks with my eyes. The way I figured it, standing there, my breath fogging on the glass, the space where we could watch the girls perform started at my waist level and stretched twenty-five, maybe even thirty feet. It stole my breath.

God.

When these girls were down here, swirling inside the mini-castle doors, I could see now that they were under tons of water—the pressure pushing down on them was enormous. It made me feel too small. Before I meant to, I'd backed away from the tank. Quickly I made my way around the glass bend and through a black cotton curtain, and there I was, backstage.

I guess I was expecting a girly locker room with lighted tables, Hollywood style. But what I found was a dark warehouse space, tall as the tank but lightless. This was where they stored back-drops for old shows.

My footsteps were loud on the wet concrete floor as I slipped between beams and old chipped flats depicting pirates, island natives with tattooed faces. A treasure chest filled with silver-painted coins and crushed-up Diet Coke cans. A dry-erase board outlined that day's show—girls' names were written next to each song title. I wondered how it would feel to see my name there.

There was a light at the rear of the building, and back there I could hear voices.

Jam-packed in a small space behind the storeroom, the mermaids had created a makeshift makeup room. Three girls quickly dug into piles of sparkling costume parts overflowing from a big picnic table into a heap on the dirty floor, while the two parking lot girls shared the light of a swing-arm desk lamp and a dingy mirror propped against a wall. The dark-haired girl smoothed on red lipstick from a chubby pencil. The blonde penciled her evil eyebrows but stopped mid-arch when she saw me. The severe, unfinished angle said angry and exotic at the same time.

"You!" she said to my face in the mirror. All movement in the room stopped as the girls looked at me, the new arrival. In the mirror over her head, I caught a glimpse of myself. Two hours in the parking lot had pushed my hair to a new level of bushy curl. Crescent-shaped sweat stains crept out from the underarms on my tank top, and my khaki shorts had wrinkles at the crotch, probably from sitting on a mossy log for two hours—and that made me not even want to look at the seat of my shorts. It was best not to know some things, really.

My face was red from excitement and heat, and I suddenly wished I'd taken five minutes that morning to put on eyeliner or cover-up—anything to keep me from looking so much like my gym teacher right at that moment.

Then, quick like that, their attention moved on. They were sorting through a heap of silky, glittery clothes, costume tops with sequins on the outside and a real swimmer's swimsuit underneath, like I wasn't even there. I was getting used to that. Being the girl who, after the initial newness wears off, just became plain. Forgettable. Which usually had the potential to set me off and make me do something stupid to get noticed, but right then, I needed the comfort of invisibility.

The girl at the mirror held out her hand for the pencils.

"Oh, right." I handed them to her, then wiped my sweaty palm on my shorts. If she noticed, she didn't say, unlike Tom, who would've made loud retching sounds.

"Thanks," she said absently.

I stepped back to the doorway just outside the dressing room and tried to blend with the shadows.

"I'm starving," said the blonde, sounding whinier than people usually sound when they say that. Had the dark-haired girl rolled her eyes just then? The first girl continued. "All I had was a Power Bar and a salad yesterday."

"So *eat,*" said the other girl.

"No dressing on it either," the blonde continued.

The brunette breathed deeply, not quite a sigh. She dabbed on a dollop of the cream blush I'd brought, which added a gorgeous sheen to her cheeks, highlighted the rich golden brown of her eyes. A quick pass of the brush through her hair left it silky smooth, the kind of straight that only a trained professional could make mine do. She got up off her knees, rolled her neck to release some tension. "I'm going to suit up." She grabbed a stack of clothes off the table and was gone out the back door into bright daylight, where I guessed the dressing rooms were.

One girl held up a green-sequined bathing suit top. "Okay, the other strap isn't here. I give up."

Another girl said, "This place is a pit."

"Look, just grab something and let's go," salad-with-no-dressing said, getting up and dusting off her knees. From the heap on the floor, she flung the girl a halter-neck top, bigger and the color of watered-down grape juice.

"Oh, niiice," sarcasm high. "Uh-uh. You wear it."

"I'm not the one who lost my strap," she said, and headed for the door. They all followed, even the last girl, who gave one last glance at the hopeless pile before she picked up the purple top with two fingers and held it at arm's length like it was a dead thing as she walked out back.

It started off, *really,* with me simply stepping back into the dressing room to look for the girl's lost strap. I was just going to be five minutes and then out of there, but soon I was sorting, organizing, putting the heaps of junk into tidy piles—hair ties, bracelets, props, bathing suit tops and bottoms in every color. Some looked to be old and unwearable, and those I stuck in a milk crate on a shelf. Found a pair of tube socks so black, I just kicked them toward the trash can to deal with later.

Every time I'd pick something up, I'd find another pile underneath and start folding, stacking. The rhythm of it became comforting.

More makeup pencils scattered around the floor. I stood them up in a foam cup.

Bangle bracelets, plastic, in varying shades of iridescent green. Each one got looped onto its own thumbtack on the corkboard.

A sheer black tuxedo jacket with tails that would trail in a swimmer's current, size medium.

A maid's apron, edged with the most delicate white eyelet.

Silly devil horns on a red satin hood.

Shaken out and hung on hangers, spaced an inch apart on the broomstick I'd hung from two ceiling beams to make a wardrobe bar.

Part of me wondered, where were the mermaid fins?

Instead, I found layers of rich, bright-colored satin that felt like liquid on my fingertips. Stitched together to form an elegant headdress Cleopatra would've worn; its gold-flecked braids would catch the light underwater. The headdress I put on the head of a giant teddy bear from the boardwalk, which got the seat of honor—the director's chair, under the desk light, admiring itself in the mirror.

And that's how I found the missing green-sequined strap—it was tied in a bow around the bear's neck. I untied it and laid it on the picnic table, otherwise cleared.

When I heard the door open again, I stood back to catch my breath and realized too late how freakishly clean I'd made the place. The three girls at the door, dripping wet, looked around, mouths agape.

Finally one said, "Okay, who *are* you?"

"My name's Amy."

She ventured further, "Do you, like, work here?"

Another girl snickered. "No, she just goes around playing cleaning fairy."

"I'm going to," I said. "Work here. I want to, anyway."

"Not this year, you won't," said salad-with-no-dressing. "Mermaid tryouts were in the spring. You missed them."

I held steady. "Well, what other jobs *do* they hire for?"

"Nothing," she said.

Dead-ended again. In the middle of the room, I'd created a pile of trash, old papers, moldy rags, and I said to them, "I was just going to throw this stuff away."

"The bins are out back."

I gathered up the mildewed pile, turning my face away from the stench. No one offered to help. I made it out back, where a line of full trash cans stood. I dumped the pile into the least full one.

Just then, the old lady I'd seen the day before cleaning up the theater appeared, her arms loaded with empty drink cups and crumpled popcorn boxes. Steely gray eyes looked sharply at me under her blunt-cut gray bangs. "Are you the one who did that to the dressing room?"

I winced, realizing my mistake too late. That was probably her job.

"Sorry," I said. I felt my head shrink down on my shoulders. A wave of nausea hit me that I would be leaving here, not only without a job, but also with people actively hating me. My eyes stung, and I prayed that I could get out before the tears spilled over.

"They said you were asking about work."

"I didn't realize," I said, gesturing toward the trash. "I was just trying to help."

"Everybody always wants to be a mermaid," she said. "If you want to be a mermaid, you're out of luck."

The confusion must have showed on my face.

"But if you want to pick up after the shows, keep the place clean, I could use a hand. I've been on Bruce for years to get some help in here."

I let all my air out in a loud burst, the tears finally officially spilling over. My nose ran like a faucet, and I was officially blubbering. The lady must've thought I was the biggest freak on the planet, crying about being asked to pick up trash at a theme park. She rolled her eyes, went on, "Five bucks an hour cash, under the table. Payday is Friday. No stealing, no smoking, no skinny-dipping."

"Thank you," I managed, finally giving in and wiping my nose with the tail of my filthy tank top.

"I'm Emma," she said, turning and walking back to the dressing room. "Welcome aboard."

When I got back to the motel, the sun was cresting into late afternoon. I scanned the courtyard for Dylan—he was nowhere to be seen. Lynne, head cocked in that where-have-you-been way, waved a curious hello from the second-floor balcony, where she was sitting with a few ladies, drinking iced tea. "I talked to your mom earlier," she called down. "She asked where you were."

I had to think fast. Lynne would kill me if she knew I'd gone way into North Wildwood—farther than that, even. She'd been clear that it was off-limits, that it would be dangerous. Breaking her trust wouldn't be a good way to start the summer. She might even send me home.

"I was looking for a job," I blurted. "Tell her I'll be waitressing at Mama Leone's on the boardwalk."

"Which one?"

"There's more than one?"

Lynne laughed, a rich sound like music. "You crack me up."

There, that was decided. Lips sealed. The park was mine. My private place that I didn't have to explain to everybody else. All day I'd sat at the back of the bleachers, watching every show, memorizing. Being around water all day and not swimming had been weird, though, and I couldn't wait to feel the coolness on my face and to warm up my muscles by slicing through the water.

I did a shallow dive into the deep end of the motel pool and started doing lazy laps to wake up my body. It had been days since my last swim, but still my muscles knew what to do. So well that I could unplug my brain and just go on autopilot.

In my mind, I replaced Lynne's pool with the giant tank. I took four, five, six powerful strokes, picturing the audience below, their chins lifted, watching me with an "ooh" on their lips. They would notice my gracefulness and wonder how I could whip around like that and make it look so effortless.

When I reached the wall, I would dive beneath the surface and curl into a whip-fast push turn—the trick I used in swim meets to push me past the other swimmers.

A girl from the other team would be chopping away at the surface, thinking she was in the lead. I'd still be underwater, still shooting through the water from the powerful shove I'd given myself off the wall. The roar of the crowd when I'd pop up suddenly in front of the leader—it made me feel like I was floating on air. It was the same feeling I got just standing in the park.

Soon I was in a rhythm.

Power launch off the wall, cross half the pool in a single breath.

At the top, four, five, six strokes, then turn, power launch, repeat.

I gulped in air with every left-handed stroke. I practiced locking my ankles together, pretending they were a single fin. It made me pull harder with my arms, but I could definitely do it. I could feel the smile tug at my lips.

After I don't know how many laps, as I was gulping in a breath, I realized I had company.

I recognized Dylan's hair first. Face obscured by the splashing water, his freestyle stroke was impeccable—pure power. I paused a beat, surprised to see him. A little thrilled at the idea that he'd been standing there watching me swim while I daydreamed.

But I was surprised to see he didn't stop swimming—just kept speeding toward the other end of the pool. My body knew that feeling: a race. Energy surged, propelling me forward, slicing into the water, finding my rhythm again. I caught up to him, and he kept pace with me easily. For now, anyway.

At the wall, I ducked under and shoved hard, keeping my hands in a tight V, chin tucked, making myself as streamlined as possible. Well beyond the halfway point, I surfaced and caught a glimpse of him.

Damn. He was two strokes ahead.

I skipped a breath and just took one every other stroke. Economizing. Ducked under at the wall, turned, shot harder this time. Let my feet kick individually instead of using them as a single fin. When I surfaced, we were neck and neck, matching strokes. His longer arms and stronger kicks edged him ahead a little, and then duck, flip turn, shoot.

My lungs were starting to burn with the effort, but I wouldn't let go. At the surface, I switched to breathing on my right stroke so I could keep an eye on him. Between breaths, I saw that he was watching, doing the same thing to me. Even swimming crazy hard like that, the smile on his face was huge, dimples and all. Air caught in my chest; I was a little nervous—it snuck up on me every time how gorgeous he was.

It was kind of funny. I think he thought so too.

We both started laughing, and he actually laughed so hard he swallowed water and started coughing, so that's when I let go of the race and stopped. Good timing. My pulse was racing. I could hear my heart pounding and blood rushing in my ears.

Water drops made his eyelashes dark and gorgeously intense. "God," he said. The way he licked his lips, I thought he might have been thinking about mine.

I smiled, gathered my hair into a bunch on the top of my head. Knew he was looking at me and maybe there was something to my face that made him want to look some more.

"So I forgot to ask yesterday—your parents just let you stay? That was cool of them," he said. I could hear he was a little winded too, like me.

"*Parent,*" I corrected quickly. I took a big breath on the sly to bring my heart rate back to normal. "Just my mom. Tom is my stepfather."

"Oh. Anyway, it's still cool of her."

"It sort of happened by accident," I said. "I freaked her out with the window thing."

He looked up at me. "Window thing?"

"Lynne didn't tell you?" He shook his head. "I broke that window up there, the big one. It was an accident. Mel and Trina were trying to get to the air conditioner, and they pushed me."

"They do a lot of pushing," he said, his voice low, looking away from me.

"Yeah," I said, loving that he sounded a little protective.

I hooked my knees over the edge of the pool. My back floated on the surface, hair fanning out. Arms loose and light. He came over right next to me, between my arm and my body, close but not touching. Just having him so close made the water feel warm, or maybe that was from the racing.

"You sound like you're sad about it."

"Do I?" My voice sounded high in my ears. "I'm not. It just happened weird. I'm happy I'm here."

It would've been nice for him to say he was happy I was still down there, even though I could already tell that he was. Still, it's nice to hear that kind of stuff. To confirm things.

The night of no sleep was catching up with me. My eyes wanted so badly to close. The swim, the park, Dylan, everything, I just wanted to lie down on the sofa bed and see what my dreams would make of this day.

I lifted my feet to let go of the concrete and let myself sink down under the water. A slow free fall. Way up there at the top, I saw Dylan watching me.

When I came up, Lynne was there. "Hey, you," she said. "I'm making some dinner. Actually, breakfast for dinner—scrambled eggs. You want some?"

Suddenly I was starving. "Ooh, yes." I hadn't eaten anything all day. I thought of salad-with-no-dressing and smiled.

To Dylan, she said, "Eggs?"

"I need to head out," he said. "Thanks, though."

We both headed across the pool to the steps, and this time he let me win. Lynne had drifted toward the door but not quite gone in, so Dylan and I just kind of laughed and he said, "I'll see you later."

As he walked away, I watched water droplets run down his shoulders to the small of his back and thought what a nice journey that must be.

CHAPTER *Ten*

INSIDE, LYNNE STOOD AT THE COUNTER. RIPE TOMATOES WERE diced into neat cubes on the butcher block, and I could smell the sweet, licoricey basil she was mincing.

"Scrambled okay? With this stuff in it?"

"Yum. Perfect," I said, sitting at one of the antique-white bar stools at the high counter.

She handed me four eggs and a bowl, and I started cracking them one at a time. "So tell me about your adventures today."

"I just ran around the boardwalk," I said. "Looking for a place to work."

"Glad to hear it paid off," she said.

"Not exactly brain surgery and the pay sucks, but hey, free pizza, right?" The lie rolled off my tongue too easily as I tossed an eggshell into the garbage disposal.

She plopped a thin slice of butter in the pan and it sizzled angrily. "Any other adventures?"

I tried hard to keep my stare blank. Was she hinting about the park?

She turned to me, a spatula in her hand. "Come on, Amy. Do you think I'm completely stupid?"

Oh God—she *knew*. How did she know?

This was a small town. She must know somebody at the park—maybe one of the ladies I'd just seen her drinking iced tea with up on the balcony. Of course. That was so stupid of me. My head hung down, heavy. Now she was going to send me home. I could feel tears welling up and was ashamed that I'd tried to fool her after everything she'd done for me.

"Oh, for God's sake." Something bonked me on the top of the head, then dropped into my lap. A cherry tomato. "You think I never had a summer romance? Besides, he's a good kid—I'm glad you guys hit it off."

I held the tomato in the palm of my hand. My confused look made her laugh.

"Blue eyes? Dimples like Swiss cheese?" She lobbed another cherry tomato at me playfully—it hit me mid-forehead, landed in my lap. "As if I wouldn't notice the sparks flying off you two."

Relief flooded over me, made my lungs start to work again. Lynne launched another tomato and another, and I started to laugh. Tossed one back at her, then another.

"Hey!" she screamed, grabbing a dish towel to swat at me. "Respect your elders!"

I got down on the cool tile floor on my hands and knees, look-ing for tomatoes, laughing.

"Amy and Dylan, sitting in a tree, K-I-S-S-I-N-G," Lynne sang.

I blurted, "I *wish*."

She swatted me on the butt with her towel. "Are you kidding me?" Then returning to her sizzling pan, "I got eyes, girl. That boy is smitten."

I sat on the floor and looked up at her, the smile on my face so big I couldn't do anything about it if I tried. "You think?"

"Amy," she said. "I don't *think*. I *know*."

Lynne and I decided to spend the next morning at the beach together. The day before, Emma had told me to be at work around two since that's when they got busiest. I would probably go early, but still, I had the whole morning to pass, and hanging out with Lynne would help it go faster.

We packed light. Two compact aluminum chairs with hot pink seats that you could carry with one finger. A liter of water on a strap. We coated ourselves in sunblock before heading down, so we left the bottle behind.

Down on the sand, we passed the early birds who'd set up camp and walked all the way down to the edge of the water. I copied Lynne, unfolding my chair right there where the surf rolled in gently after the waves broke. We both sighed when we sat down.

"This is my favorite part of the day," she said.

"You do this every day?" I closed my eyes, tilted my face up to the sun.

"I try." The water washed up, a cool gentle sheet under our heels on the sand.

"We always sit way back there," I said. "But I like this. It's nice."

"Your mom and I used to come to the beach all the time, back when she'd visit down here." Her voice dropped at the end—was that disappointment?

"You guys used to hang out a lot," I said, turning my face toward Lynne, trying to read her calm profile. They seemed so different—it was hard for me to imagine Lynne and my mom being as close as they'd supposedly been back then.

"We did," she said, eyes still closed. If she had any dirt to dish, she wasn't budging.

I wanted her to remember her good memories of *me,* too. "I remember one time you came school shopping with us," I said. "I was in second grade, and you bought me a blue raspberry Slurpee and let me ride the twenty-five-cent carousel ride, like, three times in a row."

Her laugh was low in her throat. "That's right—it was the outlet mall in Reading," she said. "Melissa was there too. She always had to be doing everything her big sister was doing."

My eyes closed, trying to picture it. In the clear memory I had, Mel was never there.

After a while, Lynne said, "Your mom was always out there, in the water."

"You both in your bikinis, probably," I said, smiling. "Were you always meeting guys out here?"

Lynne laughed. "No, your mom wasn't like that. No bikini, no flirting. She just loved to swim. Besides, she was pretty much always dating your dad back then, from the time she was fourteen, except once . . . when they broke up for a bit." She paused, her voice growing heavier on the last part. "Your mom is a one-man kind of girl," she added, lightening her tone.

I was stuck on the other thing she'd said. "They broke up? I never knew that."

Lynne shrugged. "They were young—they'd been together their whole dating lives. I don't really remember the whole story. Anyway, they were just broken up for one summer, and your mom came down here to lick her wounds. The ocean has a way of healing people, you know."

"Hmmm," I said, stretching my toes into the wet sand.

"Anyway, when your mom went back up to the city at the end of the summer, they got back together. Got married. Had you." Her quick touch on my arm was nice. "The rest is history," she said. "Your mom was always a little awkward around guys back then."

I was confused. Mom, the one who could turn any man's head? Who could coax most waiters into letting her order things that weren't on the menu, who could smile her way out of any traffic ticket? There was a time when she didn't know how to act around guys?

The Mom I knew had full certainty about men. She enjoyed them, had chosen a life that let her be in their company, whereas Melissa and I seemed to bore her or not give her enough of what she wanted. As bad as I got, I never made Mom choose between me and Tom because I had a terrible feeling about what the decision would be. In fact, hadn't I already seen just that happen? Wasn't that why I was down here still?

I blinked, pushing the thought away.. "Mom hit the jackpot with Tom, though, huh?" I said.

I heard Lynne sigh again and she paused so long, I thought she wasn't going to reply. Then she said, "This is a weird conversation to have with you, Amy." Her gaze went out to the water, more serious than I'd meant. "Your mom sees something there that makes her happy."

"Ugh." I collapsed farther back in my seat, letting my head dip back over the edge. "You're telling me you like him?"

"What I think doesn't matter—your mom deserves to be happy, and if he makes her happy, who am I to meddle?"

"He's an ass," I mumbled under my breath.

She breathed out hard. "You know what? You're an ass to him."

I sat up straighter. "Excuse me?"

"I heard you," she said. "On the steps that day. 'I'd still be smarter than your sorry ass.' Really, Amy." My cheeks burned red. She glanced away for a moment, then back. "Look, he *is* a jerk, but you make him more of a jerk. You instigate. I've seen you do it to your mom and Melissa too."

I kept my face frozen, stinging from the criticism. "What? Am I just supposed to sit there and take it?"

"No," she said. "But you need to think, could you be the one causing some of this trouble?"

I sat forward to let her know I was serious. "Parents aren't supposed to say the stuff he says," I said. My voice was a little thick and shaky, so I cleared my throat.

She gave me a minute, bending forward to splash water on her knees, arms. Cooling off a little. She finally sat back, the water glistening off her. "Amy, he's a person. Your mom's a person. You're a person. We're all responsible for what we do to each other. Being someone's kid doesn't give you amnesty. You can't be a bull in a china shop."

"I'm just defending myself," I said quickly, under my breath.

"No, you aren't. You're doing more than that and you know it."

I leaned back in my chair and slid my sunglasses on. I wondered what time it was but didn't want to ask Lynne. Soon enough it would be time to go to work.

On weekdays, the park did shows at ten, two-thirty, and eight. By the time I got there early at one, the stands were fuller than I'd seen. Two church buses in the parking lot had delivered sixty senior citizens, mixed with families whose young kids were way up at the foot of the tank, sticky cotton-candy hands pressed against the glass. A carpet of popcorn spanning three rows of bleachers—probably a food fight from restless kids attending the early show.

I grabbed the broom.

Music came on and I caught a quick glance up at the shack overhead—Bruce, the angry guy from the other day who I'd learned was actually the park's owner, was there watching me. He looked pissed to see me back. I ducked my head and set to work with the broom so he could see I was serious.

He hovered over me like that for the whole show.

When it ended and the park emptied out, I was picking up trash from each row, and Bruce barked over the loudspeaker, "You can't put cans in with the regular trash!"

I stood up fast, startled. Realizing he was yelling at me, I said, "Sorry."

"Get a box from the supply closet," came the voice from above.

I glanced around, panicked—saw a set of double doors in the hillside. Darted over to them.

"Not there!" he yelled. "The *other* supply closet." Was that sarcasm? How was that helpful? I squinted up at the control room, but inside, it was too dark to see him.

I glanced around and saw another door—this one with a sign that said SUPPLY CLOSET. Oh. My head hung lower, and I grabbed a box from the damp darkness inside.

By four-thirty, I'd picked up every piece of trash, every dirty tissue and hard-candy wrapper left by those old folks. Swept down thirty-six rows of bleachers. Peeled seventeen pieces of chewing gum off the underside of benches. Rolled in one puddle of spilled Coke while I was gum hunting, which left my white T-shirt with a stiff brownish stain. Windexed the face of the tank where the kids had been, getting it ready for the next set of sticky hands. Emptied all the trash cans and carried the overstuffed green bags out to the Dumpster in the parking lot, getting an icy glare from the redhead at the ticket counter as I passed each way.

At one point between shows, I saw some of the mermaids from the day before over behind the snack bar, grabbing handfuls of chips and sharing a cup of fruit punch.

God, how many mermaids were there? Six right there. And I remembered maybe one or two others from the other day.

I waved a casual hi, but most of them didn't see me. Only the girl with the long dark hair, the one from the parking lot, seemed to notice me. She waved hi but didn't call me over to join them.

My tongue was sticking to the roof of my mouth, I was so thirsty. But then I looked down—covered in dirt and sweat and whatever else I'd picked up from the splintered bleachers on the other side of their clear tank, I couldn't go up there. I thought I'd better keep my distance. I would have to shower and burn these clothes before I saw Dylan again. When I looked like this, I knew what guys thought. I wouldn't be making that mistake again.

Before the eight o'clock show, Emma called me over from the curtain. "Let's get you back here," she said, and I quickly stepped down to her, not sure if this was a good thing but sensing that it wasn't. "Let's not stand out there and distract people. They don't need to see us sitting around daydreaming."

So instead she put us, or me, to work backstage. She handed me a can of spray sealant that had a skull and crossbones printed on its warning label. I said, "Should I wear a mask or something?"

"No need," she said. "You're just doing these." She pointed at a row of prop pieces that were about to fall apart—a four-foot-tall clamshell and a giant American flag, both leaning against a steep set of stairs that led high into the rafters—before quickly heading out to the theater.

I took a deep inhale till it felt like my lungs would burst and held my breath. Then I sprayed. I made my mind travel outside to the show, following the music. I knew this part of the mermaid dance already by heart. I waved the spray back and forth, side to side, with the beat.

It must have been exhausting for the mermaids to swim like that for three shows a day. Too exhausting for them to have a spare breath to say hi, to hang up their wet costume tops—even to drape them over the back of a chair instead of leaving them in a damp pile on the water-stained picnic table.

Yes, it must have been very, very hard.

So I did all this a second time too, after the eight o'clock show, when everybody else had left. Hoping somebody would notice how much I'd done without complaining.

It was after ten when I was done. Walking through the warehouse behind the tank, I called out, "Hello!"

No one was there.

Everyone else had left. Nobody had even said goodbye.

My breath felt thick in my throat.

I was the new girl, I thought. After a while I'd become part of the flow there. That had to happen.

I licked my lips and listened. My heart quickened as I suddenly remembered the benefit of being alone. I wound my way through the darkness to the backstage steps, the rickety wooden things that led way up to the roof. I climbed them two at a time.

At the top, I opened the door slowly. There it was. The top of the mermaid pool, the part hidden from the audience by boats and surfers on a wooden fence.

It was bigger than I'd originally thought. Wide as a four-lane highway, deep as a two-story house. With the stage lights out, an inky black yawned up at me from just below the surface.

Depth. It was what glued my feet in place on the wooden deck.

If I dove in, I could slip too deep. All that water's weight would push on my chest, steal my breath. Keep me down there.

I took a step closer to the edge and looked down. I could see my own outline in the shifting water.

Down there was where the show happened. Where my hair would billow in a sleek trail as I made people remember a fairy tale that they had forgotten all about.

Everyone on the bleachers, they would want to be me.

To be in the tank, where I was better than I was on dry land. Where storybooks weren't just fantasy.

I suddenly wished Dylan were there with me so he could feel the magic of this place.

The moonlight shifted, bathing the top of the pool in a warm white light. I closed my eyes and breathed in, promising it to myself.

I would be in there. I had to be.

CHAPTER *Eleven*

FRESH SPRING WATER. THAT WAS WHY MERMAID PARK SMELLED so green and alive. The park sat on a natural mineral spring whose water flowed into the tank. A deep, cool freshwater stream took the used water as it flowed out of the park and away through the woods.

I learned this from a tri-fold color brochure I found while dusting the gift counter.

A handmade poster on the wall said, ELVIS WAS HERE! 1953. And you could have a photo postcard that proved it, for just ninety-nine cents. President Eisenhower had apparently visited once, too. A yellowing newspaper clipping over the register showed him in front of the tank, with a mermaid behind him underwater, an I Like Ike button pinned to her chest.

I'd come to work early that day to see the first show, tired of sitting around the motel. Last night after work, I'd hung out in the motel courtyard till after midnight, hoping Dylan would stop by. I kept expecting him to show up next to me in the pool and challenge me to a race. Or to call to me from the roof and invite me up. I'd even climbed to the top of the roof stairs and peeked out to make sure he wasn't around.

Not that we'd had plans. I guess I'd been hoping he would have just reserved that time for me. Disappointment kept me silent and bored. Going to bed at 2 a.m., I wished I could have gone right then right to the park.

I managed to wait until ten-thirty to arrive. Seeing me there, Bruce had said, "You only get paid starting at two o'clock."

I nodded quickly. "I know." I flushed, realizing too late how kiss-uppy I sounded. The red-haired girl from the ticket counter snorted out a fast laugh as she walked past on her way to the snack counter. I felt my shoulders rise self-consciously. On the way back, she glanced at me over her shoulder and let her empty straw wrapper drop to the ground.

I glared hard at the back of her head, then went to pick it up before Bruce saw it. He was in the control room above, replacing a shorted-out speaker.

So far that day, I'd raked gravel to cover dirt patches in the parking lot and helped Bruce unload snack bar supplies from his truck, during which time he managed to not say a single word to me. I felt my sweaty fingers straining to hold on to the two-gallon tub of ketchup and for a moment thought how Dylan would probably be the kind of guy to take this from me and carry it. But when I slid it onto the counter and heard Bruce clear his throat and say, "Good," I had to push my lips together to keep my laugh from bubbling out all over the place.

One of the mermaids, Stephanie—the nice one with the dark hair—had even noticed how good the theater looked, giving it an impressed whistle as she passed through.

Between the afternoon and evening shows, I buzzed from chore to chore. Bruce had backed away from me slowly when he found me scrubbing down the soap dispensers in the men's bathroom. Emma had stopped seeking me out to ask me to clean this, organize that. Buried deep in the supply closet, stacking the boxes by size, I'd heard her call in, "I bet your bedroom is spotless."

Ha. My bedroom back home resembled the scene of a burglary. Whole drawers emptied onto the floor. Unmade bed, lampshade askew. Shoe box dioramas from Rob under the bed—one to mark each monthly anniversary. Three alarm clocks, each in a different spot far from where I slept—the only way I didn't miss school.

But this place *deserved* my help.

It was nine-thirty by the time everyone left Mermaid Park that night. I stood at the bottom of the bleachers, facing the darkened tank. The reflection looking back was ragged, my arm holding empty soda cups against my stomach. Both hands gripping empty popcorn boxes tighter than I'd meant to. When I licked my cracked lips, I tasted the salt of dried sweat. My stomach was tight with fear.

Tonight I had to go at least as far as last night. Farther. Once I got past the just-getting-in part, it would be easy from there.

My feet were light and fast as I went up, up, up the steps and out on the deck. Right up to the edge of the pool before I even let myself stop and think.

From up here, it looked like some of the smaller lights had been left on, giving some shape to the objects that'd been pure shadow last night. Funny, I thought it had been pitch-dark a few minutes ago.

So I guess that helped. I stepped out of my flip-flops and sat on the edge, slipping my feet in.

The coldness of the water was startling. How did the mermaids perform in this? I guess they got used to it, but for some reason I'd expected it to be warmer.

Before I could stop and think, I hefted my weight onto my hands and let my body slide into the pool in one smooth drop. I paid attention to the sped-up beat of my heart, listening for problems as water filled my shorts pockets, made my white tank billow, crept under my bra—first the sting of cold. Then, a moment later, numbness made it better. One hand stayed gripped tight on the edge. Breaths came short and fast.

I lowered my chin to my chest and looked down into the water. Shapes, colors, so clear from the bleachers, were all just shifting blurs up here. I saw my feet scrambling below, looking for something to hold on to—which there wasn't, for much too far for me to think about.

My hand gripped the edge, wanting to pull myself out. I focused hard on my fingers, white-knuckled from my strong hold.

My eyes filled. My teeth started to chatter.

My arms didn't want to hold me, tired from a day of working and hauling. My breath came quicker as I thought if I stayed here much longer, I wouldn't be *able* to pull myself out.

There it was. The out. The quitting.

I had spent hours staring into the tank with a focus I didn't know I had. Yet there it was again, the same ending as everything else I did. Me, quitting.

Forget that.

I grabbed a deep breath and before I could change my mind, I ducked under the surface. My feet kicked out, looking for something to contact. Water rushed into my ears, then hissed, then silence—a not unpleasant deafness. I let a stream of breath out of my nose, testing it—the bubbles danced past my eyelids, and that reminded me to open my eyes.

I was in there, my hair floating all around my face.

My eyes went big, hungry to take it all in. The pirate ship-wreck—from above it had no deck. The seaweed strands were only painted green on the front. It was so different.

Floating up at the top like this, I knew that no one in the bleachers would be able to see me—but if they could, what I would look like?

Like two nights ago in the pool, when Dylan had watched me from above. I had felt pretty.

I cast my eyes up, remembering the feeling.

Wait—I was seeing things. Hallucinating because I didn't have enough air.

It was like I could actually *see* Dylan, standing right there on the edge of the tank. I came to the surface, gasping for air, and blinked.

There he was for real. Dylan.I rubbed my eyes, waiting for the familiar chlorine sting, but there was none. I suddenly remembered where I was—the park and not the pool. Panic filled my chest, and my breaths sounded short and ragged to my ears. "Who told you I was here?" I hoped he couldn't hear the thickness in my voice, which always gave me away when I was about to cry.

"Nobody," he said. He squatted down to one knee, coming down to me. "Why *are* you here?"

I cleared my throat, waited for it to open. Noticed that he had drawn his brows together in confusion. The tightness in my chest eased a little. Confusion meant he really *hadn't* known I was going to be here, and that meant no one else knew yet either—Lynne, Mom.

"Wait, why are *you* here?" I said.

"I clean the tank. For the owner." For the first time, I noticed the long-handled brush he had in his hand. Extension poles lay on the deck behind him. "Are you supposed to be here? Did you break in?"

"No," I said.

"Because I can just say you're here with me."

"No, it's okay," I said. "I'm kind of working here too. Not doing this." I splashed some water. I breathed out hard, waiting to hate the sound of it. "I take out the trash."

He nodded, untouched by it. "So the pizza place thing you told Lynne?"

I shrugged, caught. "I guess I lied."

"Why?"

"She told me walking around on this side of town was like wearing a sign that said, 'Murder me, please.' She made me swear to stay south of Twentieth Street."

"I don't know—maybe it used to be sketchy," he said. "But it's safe enough now. Weird."

"Well, she was pretty adamant. She'd kill me. Promise me you won't tell Lynne," I said, pulling myself up a little on the edge, closer to him so he could tell I was serious.

He paused. In his eyes, I could see shades of shifting blue. I reached out and touched his knee; his jeans were old ones, softer than a T-shirt.

Finally, he shook his head, laughing. "I won't say anything," he said.

I took a big breath. I was lucky he was like that, so loyal to me.

Under the jeans, he wore black board shorts that sat low on his slim hips. I held the brush while he jumped in. "Want to help?" he said.

"Can I?"

"I just brush the scunge off the windows," he said, taking the brush and sliding it down the interior of the tank. He went hand over hand with the pole, the muscles in his arms flexing with the effort, and brought the brush head up to show me. Sure enough, soft green threads clung to the bristles.

"What *is* that?" I treaded water, coming closer to look.

"It's just algae," he said. He took a thread in his hand.

"Uck," I said. Up close, I could see all of its slimy hairs.

He laughed. "What do you think you're swimming in? Champagne?"

I dipped my fingertips in the water and flicked it at him.

He shook it off, then lifted the algae strand toward me.

"Don't even think about it," I said, laughing, swimming backward away from him along the edge. His goofy boldness was fun.

He swam after me one-armed, dangling the slimy algae toward me. In a menacing voice, he said, "Attack of the killer algae!"

"Dylan! Ew—help!" I swam away from him in a few fast strokes out to the middle of the tank.

He stayed where he was, just watching me. I could see his silhouette in the light from the top of the steps.

I laughed. "You scare me when you get quiet like that."

I heard him take a deep breath. "Do you have a boyfriend?" he asked.

I smiled. "No." My heart sped up. "Currently boyfriend-less."

"Why?"

I shrugged, suddenly glad for the darkness—I couldn't tell him about the Rob thing, explain how I'd been so into a craft-making, scrapbooking-type guy. And the Brian thing—that story would never cross my lips with anyone. "Why don't you have a girlfriend?"

He was moving toward me gradually. My breaths were coming

quicker than before. "I just don't," he said. "I dated somebody last year, but it kind of ran out of . . . oomph."

How could anyone run out of anything with him? "Hate when it runs out of oomph."

"Yes, you definitely need oomph," he said.

Close now, I could see his lips, and I was amazed to think that I might kiss them sometime soon. I smiled at the thought. He smiled too.

"You're smiling," I said.

He looked down, shy. "That's because I know something," he said.

My heart pounded. I looked up at him, chanced a glance at his lips. "What? What do you know?"

"I know," he said, "that you can't hide."

"I can't?"

"No—you can't hide from this," he said, bringing his hand up to my face, I thought to hold my chin while he kissed me. I had a flash of the Mexican soap opera—I knew what this led to next.

I was about to close my eyes when he lifted his other hand in front of me. The drippy green strands took a moment to regis- ter—it was an oozing handful of pond slime.

I half screamed, half laughed. "Nooo!" I said, swimming back- ward away from him, fast, splashing water at him with my feet.

"You cannot hide from the deadly algae."

Now I was using both my hands and feet to kick up water, blinding him. He reached out and grabbed my feet, and I shrieked. He pulled me closer to him, his smooth arms radiating warmth in the water around me, which didn't seem cold at all anymore.

We were both breathing hard.

Droplets hung from the front of his hair, just dangling there over his eyebrows. I reached out to catch a drop as it fell and touched his face instead.

My stomach flip-flopped.

His fingers found mine underwater and it was like they decided all on their own to intertwine and hold tight.

All I could look at were his lips, which I thought were probably thinking about coming toward mine, while right now, back at home, Mel was hiding in her room thinking of more make-believe friends she could steal from other people's memories.

Suddenly right there, his face close to mine. His lips pressed against mine hard, then softer.

My arm wound up over his shoulder and into his hair, and I felt his lips smile against mine. I smiled too.

I slid my arms around his neck in a slippery hug. I wanted to hold all this in and remember it, his arms encircling my waist, the stubble of his chin against my smooth one. How I felt like floating when he whispered into my ear, "I'm really glad you stayed this summer."

My lips were still tingling. I pressed them together, sliding them back and forth, my face just inches from Dylan's. I could feel his eyes on me, looking at my features as if he were memorizing them. This close, I always found it hard to keep eye contact, so instead I closed my eyes.

I felt him lean close to my ear. "You're so pretty, Amy," he said.

My breath came out in a shy laugh. I was grateful my eyes were closed—he couldn't see that tears had started to build there. I never knew what to do after this part, how to make whatever came next better than the perfect moment that had just happened.

Was it inevitable that everything went downhill from here?

"Your teeth are chattering," he said. "It might be time to go."

I nodded, grateful.

We ducked underwater and gave a hard shove off the wall, propelling ourselves fast toward the deck. I opened my eyes to take it all in, the fuzzy-looking castle below, the strong arms stroking in the water next to me.

A tug at my hair made me glance left. Dylan, playing.

I pushed harder with my arms, gave myself an extra kick, and surged ahead. That was how I liked it—him chasing me while I swam free.

CHAPTER *Twelve*

THAT NIGHT, I HAD A HARD TIME SLEEPING. EVERY TIME I'D CLOSE my eyes, on the insides of my eyelids, I'd see the kiss play out again. Dylan, with his weirdly worshippy gaze, looking after me—my stomach would flip-flop and send a funny taste up to my mouth. It wasn't what I'd expected to feel after finally kissing him. I didn't even really know *what* I felt, just that something was . . . off.

After a whole night of churning, I finally gave up and went to work. I was venturing out the back door of the dressing room and into an overgrown yard, looking for a spot to eat lunch where Bruce wouldn't glare at me and where it wouldn't be so obvious I was eating by myself again, when I rounded the corner to the back side of the tank and found a shed made of corrugated plastic walls, once a deep blue, bleached to sky color by the sun. Peeking in, I saw mermaid fins. *This* was where they were kept. Light flecked off their sequins, and I thought they looked so beautiful, alive, even folded over plastic tubes and left to dry.

On the shed floor was the entrance to a water-filled tube. Like a chute. Four feet wide and bending off in the direction of the mermaid pool.

The girls must get into their fins back here, then swim down through the chute—that was how they appeared from the bottom of the tank instead of the top.

It wasn't magic at all. Or at least, now I was *in* on the magic. It was still amazing—but now, I had found the clubhouse. I knew some of their *secrets*.

And then I learned another important thing. A big one.

I was in the dressing room when the girls finished the eight o'clock show—I figured I'd try to grab the costume parts before they had a chance to lose straps or toss them in the trash, where I'd found a bikini top yesterday. Keeping to the side of the dressing room, picking up items as each of the six girls tiredly dropped them, I barely made noise. I wouldn't have been surprised if they hadn't known I was there.

"Was it just me, or were there like ten people in the audience?" This from the red-haired girl at the ticket counter, Heather—she was always like that on nights like tonight, when they didn't do her starring number, some song from *The Little Mermaid*. More than once, I'd considered an anonymous letter to Disney, suggesting a cease-and-desist order.

"Were there even that many?" said the too-thin blonde from the parking lot, using a tissue and Vaseline to remove the greasy makeup. "I think Bruce should call it off for anything less than twenty-five people. I mean, come on." Stitching from the fin's heavy-gauge zipper had left its imprint up the back of her left thigh, angry and red on her fair skin.

"Oh! And there's something messed up with the air hose down by the treasure chest. It almost blew my head off when I used it."

They kept talking back and forth, but all I could think was, *Air hose?*

There were air hoses down there?

Between the tube I'd found earlier in the shed and now this, I was shaking. My own stupidity could be pretty embarrassing sometimes, but so long as nobody knew about it, I was safe.

I clenched my teeth to get my chin to stop trembling. It was dumb to be disappointed—the logical part of me had known better all along. These girls were under thirty freaking feet of water. Of course they'd need an air supply down there.

It made sense.

And right then, a thought hit me—air hoses meant it wasn't magic. It meant that anyone could do it. Well, anyone who could swim.

And I could swim.

I slipped between the girls as they changed, picking up wet veils and delicate headbands that would've been trampled and bent otherwise, wanting to help them wrap up for the night, so I could see this for myself.

Three nights straight I tried to find the hoses. Three long nights and nothing.

By the end of the third night, I was on my one-hundredth time wishing for my swim team goggles, which were at home hanging over my doorknob. I couldn't see a thing, and the next day I planned to use my lunch break to find a sporting goods store and buy some.

I'd dive down, get about eight feet, and feel behind the props—a tall strand of fake seaweed, the shipwreck. I could hear the sound of my heart pounding in my ears. Then I'd only have three or four seconds of feeling around frantically for a hose before I'd dart for the surface, worrying I might not have enough air to get back in time.

Down there, the temperature dropped. I lost all traces of the dim light from the top of the stairwell. It was just me, under a thousand pounds of water, my chest crushing inward from the pressure, my ears squeaking in protest at the icy water trying to force its way into my head.

Blackness below, so dark it was like drifting in space.

And then I'd dart for the top.

It was all I could think about.

I came home so late at night, I would quietly make my way to the side door into Lynne's apartment instead of going through the courtyard. If Dylan was up on the roof or at the pool, I really didn't have the energy to be good company.

Each night, I crawled weak-legged into the sofa bed, pressing my face into the down pillow—maybe stopping to notice, Oh, was this pillowcase embroidered with tiny tulips? Or plain with heavy satin trim, like royalty?—before falling into a deep, still sleep.

My dreams were filled with mermaids.

Saturdays were enormous, at least by Mermaid Park standards. The energy crackled in the air.

The first show wouldn't start until eleven, and it was an extended one where the kids could talk to the mermaids afterward. Backstage, the girls would slip out of their fins, then run around to a picnic table curtained off from the gift shop, where they'd zip back in and signal for the curtain to be opened so they could sign autographs, pose for pictures. This created a buzz. The girls felt like celebrities, and therefore Saturdays were the only days where they would gather, serious-minded and on time, to rehearse before the show.

July's bright white skies and damp heat had lifted, at least. The day's goodness was contagious—even Bruce, in the control room, had kept music playing for the rehearsal. The cheap speakers crackled at maximum volume, buzzing when the bass got too loud.

I climbed up on the deck above the tank to find a breeze. Hands behind my head, face up to a sky the color of Downy fabric softener and April freshness. I guessed that was probably why they called it sky blue. And once the breeze got going, you barely even noticed the mildew smell.

Puffs of clouds chugged around, lazy, like they were being

pulled on strings. Down in the water, flecks of mermaid sequins caught the light, rhythmic, then circular—the girls tightening up their act.

Suddenly, I knew something was wrong. Definitely wrong. Because one of the mermaids, Deena, broke the surface of the water at the *top* of the tank, up where I was.

That just didn't happen.

"Oh my God!" she gasped, swimming frantically for the side. Eyes wild, panic in them—I could see it. "Get me out of here!"

I grabbed her hand. In one of those moments of fear where you learn how strong you can be, she reached up, and I pretty much pulled her right out of the water and onto the splintering, moldy deck.

What was going on?

A shiny black creature flopped to the top of the pool. About four feet long and as thick as my upper arm. Snakelike. What was that?

On the far side of the tank, the mermaid with dark hair, Stephanie, surfaced. "Deena! It's just an eel. Help me get it out!"

Deena crawled farther from the edge of the pool. The eel flopped and splashed at her. "Screw that!" she said with a shiver. "That thing touched me." Then to me: "Just scoop it out with the skimmer and dump it over the edge."

I was so out of practice of being spoken to, I didn't say what I was thinking: *But that'll kill it.* And then I remembered what had happened with the horseshoe crab on the beach that night with

Mel and Trina. My hand went down to my knee, looking for the scratches that weren't there anymore.

Stephanie swam closer. "No, we just need to chase him back down the overflow tube where he came in. I'll hold the vent open. You swim toward the little guy."

From Deena, flat, humorless, "You have *got* to be kidding."

Finally Stephanie gave up on her, looked at me. "All you have to do is move toward it—trust me, it will run. It's scared of us, and it wants to go home. I promise you." Her wide-set eyes, a deep shade of brown, were heavy with seriousness.

The eel made lazy S curves underwater, back and forth, trapped. I slipped off my flip-flops and stood at the edge and decided that this time I wouldn't run. "Where's the vent? Where are we chasing him to?"

Stephanie pointed to a large metal grid down about twelve feet. "Down there. I'll slide the vent aside." Before saying anything else, she took a deep breath, dunked, and shot in that direction.

The whole tank sat half into the hillside, and that spot was where the overflow pool out back caught the extra water that couldn't fit in the tank. The spring underneath constantly flowed. When it got too full, the vent sent some water out to the pool, then from there out to the stream. But I guess stuff could swim *in* that way too. That was where the eel had come in.

I had to move before I could think too much. I dove right in, straight at the space next to that sucker, black and glossy in the sunlight. When I opened my eyes, the eel was *right freaking there,* right in the space next to my face. It darted away, and I was shocked at how fast it could move, like a whip, really.

Stephanie, down below me, was sliding the vent up, creating a wide four-foot-square goal.

The eel had moved when I'd swum straight at it. That must be the key. I surfaced for a quick breath, then dove at it with my arms outstretched in a V to keep it between my hands.

It worked. The eel dove right for the exit, take-a-picture kind of perfect.

Probably down ten feet now. The pressure on my eardrums, my chest, was intense, but I was okay.

Right when it was about to go through, for some reason it veered to the right, toward Stephanie. Maybe it was distracted by the air hose she was holding to her lips. When the eel took a wide S turn toward her, I panicked and kicked forward, thrusting my arm out, and damn if that thing didn't bump its nose right into my arm before, shocked, it veered left and darted out the hole.

I shot to the top, feeling like my head was about to explode, and breathed in air greedily. When I brought my forearm above the water, there wasn't even a mark. I let out a whoop of excitement.

Deena was still flat on the deck in her mermaid fin. "You're insane," she said.

And yeah, I guess I did look insane, so that was just funnier. When I heard a sound behind me, I swished around with panic again—but this time it was just Stephanie, and she was laughing right along with me.

"Close one," she said.

"Oh my God, I can't believe we just did that," I said.

"Nice eel wrangling, Amy."

"Thanks." I laughed, feeling my heartbeat come back to normal. Relief flooded over me in a big cool wave.

Stephanie's heaping, drippy spoonful of Dairy Queen Blizzard, vanilla with Reese's peanut butter cups, made it most of the way to her mouth before spilling. "Oops," she said, mouth full, licking it off her arm. I just smiled. I was realizing she was like that, pretty much never embarrassed.

The crowd on the boardwalk didn't notice anyway. Between the tourists and the working people like us, the place was crowded. Rollerbladers would whip by. Bicyclists too, but my back was usually turned to those—I only had a short while for lunch anyway, and I didn't want to have to blow off Stephanie if I ran into Dylan, which somehow, I kind of hoped I wouldn't anyway.

Stephanie's long shiny hair was piled into a casual-messy twist, held in place with a tortoiseshell clip. She was only two inches taller than me but weighed less, and her honey golden skin made her limbs long, lean, graceful. She was eighteen and on her third summer at the park. In two months, she would be going to college.

Every day that week, we'd ended up here between the afternoon and evening shows.

That day, she'd told me about her brother, Steven—"Steven and Stephanie, cute, right?" with a big eye roll. "And not twins, either, so my parents have no excuse." She said he was an artist, amazing, and away at school in north Jersey, near New York. And that they were close-close.

Instead of telling her about Mel, I told her about my Burger King application—ran through my long list of experience and quasi references. By the end, Stephanie was openmouthed, laughing.

"Wow, you've got guts," she said. "But I guess it's a good thing you blew that. You would've been even more miserable making french fries all summer. Although it *would* mean free fries."

"What do you mean, *more* miserable?" I asked.

"Miserable. Unhappy. As in, not happy."

I sat up straighter. "But I'm totally happy at the park."

"Really?" She frowned. "Well, I guess I get that now—at least, that you're not really miserable. But before I got to know you, I would've never believed you had a kooky, spontaneous bone in your body. You know how you are."

"No, tell me," I said. "Maybe I don't know."

"You're just so serious, the way you carry yourself, head down, eyebrows like this." She made a serious face. A vertical line creased her brow. "So *heavy* all the time."

"Tell me how you really feel," I said, trying to lighten it up.

"You asked. I told." She said it in an easy, clipped way, but there was kindness in her tone, hands up in a gesture of surrender. After a moment, she added, "You hide behind this wall." One of her hands went back and forth in front of her face, dividing us. "Why do you do that?"

In my head, I could see my mom, cool and always in her own head.

"It's just what I do. I think it's a survival skill in my family."

"Well, your family isn't here this summer. . . ."

"So time for the ice queen to defrost," I said, finishing where she'd trailed off.

"I wouldn't call you an ice queen, but yeah, a little defrosting couldn't hurt."

Late at night, I was living a different life. I was still trying for the hoses but having no luck.

I just couldn't make it down as far as I had when I'd helped Stephanie chase the eel away. In fact, it was getting worse each day. Even with my new goggles, I couldn't find the hoses.

It was three days after the eel incident, and here I was, frustrated yet again. I swam for the surface, out of breath, feeling a mixture of panic, freezing, and generally hating myself for being such a chicken. On this last try, I hadn't even reached the top of the fake seaweed.

That was it. I climbed out and collapsed on the rotting deck, hugging my stomach and trying not to cry.

Suddenly I heard a sound, someone approaching. I jerked up and looked, feeling something clench inside me when I saw who it was. Dylan, coming up the steps. No brush in his hand this time.

"Hey, stranger," he said, too loud for this quiet place. He sounded so excited to see me.

My stomach tightened. I was still catching my breath, still furious at myself. I really hadn't figured out how I felt about the kiss the other night—if I'd even liked it, how I felt about him *clearly* liking it so much. Part of me figured, anybody who could like me that much that quickly must be really, totally screwed up himself.

After a beat, I said, "Hi."

If he was going to hug me, my unenthusiastic hello changed his mind. I started putting on my shoes.

"I haven't seen you," he said. "I've been around Lynne's place, but she says you've been working all the time. So I thought I'd come by." The casual, teasing tone I'd loved so much a week ago had changed—now I definitely detected a note of pleading, questioning in his voice. An image of Rob flitted through my mind, building shoe box dioramas and drawing pictures of my toes. Every guy who liked me turned out to be a head case.

"Yeah, I've been here." My hair hung in long clumps down each side of my face and I needed to blow my nose. I could feel him watching me and had to wonder, what could he possibly see that kept him here, interested?

"We could go out to the boardwalk—you haven't been on any of the rides yet," he said. "Or we can do whatever. Your call."

My call. If it were up to me, I'd dive in that tank and get the air hose. Nothing else would make me happier. That was the only thing in the world I wanted or needed right now.

I shot a tired glance up at him.

In the dim yellow light from the stairway, I saw him in a new way—all these pieces that didn't work. The slightly overlapping front teeth, the eyes too close together, ears protruding too much.

How had I missed all this before?

"I'm tired," I said quietly, not meeting his eyes. "I'm just really, really tired." I felt a little bad for him. Embarrassed. There was mud on the toe of my shoe, and I focused intently on scraping it onto the deck.

He shifted from foot to foot. "Are you okay?" he asked, sounding concerned.

"Yeah," I said, and just left it there, hanging.

"You sound beat," he said. "Look, I'll run, but maybe another night we can do something?"

I said, "I don't know. Maybe. Or . . . maybe not." Still sitting down, not able to get myself to stand, even though he seemed to be waiting for me to get up. I couldn't even look at him because I knew how sad he'd look—that kind of puppy sad that said, *But (sniff, sniff) I really* liked *you!*

He stood there for a minute, then just turned and walked down the stairs. After I heard him go all the way down, I lay back on the deck. The wood was hard beneath my head, but I didn't care.

It was amazing what a failure I could be, even with a whole new beginning.

And the only thing sadder than being a fast failure was to be the idiot stupid enough to fall for one.

CHAPTER *Thirteen*

STEPHANIE AND I SAT UP ON THE DECK, IN A CORNER OF SHADE. A light wind kept the gnats away, mostly. I'd brought a bottle of nail polish, an iridescent silvery blue, and was carefully brushing it on my toenails. Stephanie watched through half-closed eyes.

"Do you ever get scared down there, swimming so deep?" I asked her, trying to sound casual.

"Not really," she said. "There are air hoses all around. All I have to do is swim over and breathe."

"But what if you can't get to the air hose in time?"

"I just do. We all do."

"Always? I mean, has anybody ever—has anyone died here?"

She paused a beat. "No, not the mermaids. They're strong swimmers, and we're all in there together. We may not all love each other, but if somebody gets in trouble, the other girls help."

"So some girls have gotten in trouble before?"

"Well, yeah. Some of us are a little stronger than the others." Not boasting. Just matter-of-fact.

"You're really good in there." I figured she knew this, but I knew how it was, always nice to have things confirmed. "I mean, I've watched it enough to see. You stand out."

She smiled. "Thanks. I think people can sense it when somebody's doing something they love. I definitely love it."

I tried to come up with something to offer, something I was that good at, but I came up empty. How self-pitying and pathetic was that? So I said, "I can fake-sneeze really well."

She smiled, opened one eye. "You're kidding me."

Ah, a challenge. I held up a finger, wait—as I looked up at the sun, like someone who was just about to sneeze. Held a long pause, mouth open, building suspense. Then, "Choo!" with the full effect, a little spit spray and everything.

"That wasn't fake," she said, serious.

I did it again—the gaze up, the pause, "Choo!"

"Oh my God," she said, starting to laugh. "Do it again!"

A double this time. "Achoo! Choo!" She was howling now, harder with each sneeze.

Three more sneezes and Stephanie was laughing so hard, I couldn't even keep a straight face to sneeze. Then someone clearing their throat startled me quiet. Emma, at the top of the stairs. How long had she been watching?

"Amy, if we're not too busy, the trash needs to go out to the Dumpster."

Stephanie managed a straight-faced, "Watch it, Emma—I think Amy's coming down with a cold. A bad one."

To prove it, I sneezed.

When Emma said, "God bless you," Stephanie and I collapsed into laughs. I thought I might pee my pants.

Downstairs, I must've come to the dressing room on quiet feet. Some of the girls inside were goofing around—one of them had the gold-veiled headdress on and was doing an elaborate, silly dance, hopping from foot to foot.

Deena and two other girls were sitting at the picnic table, shushing each other as they laughed. "Heather, you are so retarded," one said.

"Shh!" Deena said, frantic, looking back at the dark space where I was out of view. "Miss Sensitivity might hear you."

"Oh, what, because of her brother, the retard? Don't worry, she isn't even around."

I stood up straighter, sucking in air in surprise. Stephanie's brother? Steven was retarded?

Wouldn't Stephanie have mentioned that? Maybe they meant that he was a dork or, like, socially retarded—neither of which matched the picture of Steven in my head. But who knew? Maybe he was. I'd probably been called retarded before too.

Either way, I was glad Stephanie wasn't there. She was right— not all of them liked each other, and these girls were getting ugly—probably because they were jealous of her, the one Bruce liked best. The best mermaid at the park.

I didn't really know what to do. My first impulse was to walk in there and toss some sharp comments their way, but I kept thinking lately: *Defrost.* My new mantra.

So instead I just strolled in and said, "Hey, guys."

"Hey," they said in unison, sounding a little guilty.

"Have a good show," I said as I headed out the door. "Break a fin."

A couple of them laughed. I heard someone say, "Thanks." And I felt a little bigger, with only a small twinge of something underneath.

I didn't know why I'd said yes when Stephanie asked me to go to the cookout at Bruce's house.

"You have to come," she'd said.

"If he wanted me to come, he would've invited me," I argued. "The man has said, like, ten words to me all summer. And half of them were yelled."

She laughed. "He's not like that. He doesn't invite anybody. We just all show up every year."

"He hates me," I said, still stung from earlier that week, when he'd screamed at me for cleaning the filthy control room. I'd almost killed myself rushing down the ladder—and I was starting to wonder if that had been his intention. "He wants me gone. I can tell."

"He doesn't hate you," she'd said. "You guys are actually a lot alike."

"Please."

"You are. You're both misunderstood serious types," she said,

that furrow between her brow letting me know I was being imper-
sonated. "And you both have those cute ski-slope noses. And you
both fry like bacon when the sun comes out."

"Okay, enough with the compliments," I said flatly. "My head
is getting big."

Stephanie just laughed and circled me in a half hug. "Come
with me. It'll be fun."

I had a quick thought—would Dylan be there? I said, "Is it
just the girls from the park?"

"Just us," she said. "And your long-lost soul mate Bruce."

So that's how I ended up in the passenger seat of her rusting
Honda, headed five miles or more down this two-lane rural road,
the farthest I'd been from the motel and Wildwood all summer. It
occurred to me that Lynne would probably like to know where I
was going, that I was headed out of town and not just at the
boardwalk, but that would invite more questions, which would
mean more lying, which really was a bad thing to do. So instead I
just got in the car and went.

"Ready?" Stephanie said. We were in front of Bruce's, a one-
story brick house atop a sloping lawn that was still clinging to a
shade of near green, a trouper in the July heat. But that wasn't the
thing that had me dumbstruck. Behind this regular everyday house
on the fringe of North Wildwood, in the acres of cornfields, a giant
telecom tower loomed—a steel skeleton as tall as ten houses, a TV
antenna on steroids. So out of place here in the middle of
nowhere. And pretty much smack-dab in Bruce's backyard.

I started working on a crack about how he must get all the local stations—from China, but then I remembered, this was where the guy who hated me lived, and an icy feeling came over me.

Stephanie grabbed her purse and closed the car door. Why had I come again? I was suddenly deciding to stay put. "You coming?" she said.

"I'll be in," I said.

She shrugged and turned, heading up the driveway. And watching her go, that's when I got a weird sense of déjà vu—as Stephanie walked away from me, her stride was purposeful and casual at the same time, in her denim skirt and straw sandals with little ribbon ties around the ankles.

The memory hit me, hard.

That girl from the boardwalk, the girl who'd passed by those guys who were dying to talk to her, back a month ago now, when I thought I was still on vacation down here.

Oh my God. That girl had been Stephanie.

Sitting in the passenger seat, staring out the window at her, it finally sank in: this whole summer, it was all just meant to be.

So what was I doing still sitting there?

"Hey, wait for me!" I shouted, climbing out of the car and bounding up the driveway to meet her.

Bruce's house was a Mermaid Park museum. As everyone else milled around under shade trees out back, eating hot dogs and potato salad, Stephanie gave me the guided tour.

Newspaper clippings in a thick book, all of them yellowing with age: an article, "Glorious Maids of the Deep," dated 1958. A photo spread of their Fourth of July show, with a mermaid in an Uncle Sam beard, from 1976. An action shot of a mermaid in a fancy headdress, like the one in the dressing room. The caption read, *Mermaid Park's annual end-of-season show, the Mermaid Queen.*

I pointed to it. "Do they still do this every year?"

"Yes," she said. "It's the last song of the last show of the season. Same exact routine as back then too. I think it's kind of nice."

"I do too," I said. Then, pointing to the woman in the fancy headdress picture, "Who's the queen?"

"That one there, that was Emma," she said.

I took a closer look at the picture. The resemblance was there, just barely.

"But who does it now?" I asked.

"The last queen teaches one person the routine when she's leaving the park," she said. "There's this special turn thing that's tricky to learn, so it has to be handed down like that, from one person to another. Anyway, the last queen, for some reason, picked me. Two years ago, she taught me. I did the show for the first time last summer."

I was proud for her. That explained the jealousy in the girls' voices in the dressing room. But she didn't need to know about that.

On a wall in the dimly lit hallway was a chaotic collection of group photographs, dating from the 1950s. They were all out of order, yet each year, a group of girls stood hip to hip in front of the same tank, wearing the bathing suit style of the time— straight-cut legs in the fifties, teensy hip-hugger bottoms in the seventies. I found a shot from two years ago, 2003, and there was Stephanie, back then just my age now. Hair blunt cut in a bob and looking off somewhere to the left—the only face not seeking out the camera, yet somehow, the one you ended up looking at anyway.

I sought out years I could place. This one, down in the last row by the floorboard, 1994—where was I then? That was my first year in kindergarten, the mermaids with the high hair the eighties had made famous. The year I was born, 1989, I couldn't find, and I couldn't find the year before either in the dusty, disorganized collection on the wall. Looking for more, I went into the next room.

And there, a picture caught my eye.

It was an old high school graduation portrait, a cute guy, fair-skinned, crazy hair—could this be Bruce as a kid? No, I could tell this was too recent for that. I called to Stephanie, "Who's this?"

She came around the corner and drew a breath. Looked out the window to make sure Bruce was still in his spot behind the grill. "Bruce's son. His name was Harold, but everyone called him Skip."

"Was? Past tense?"

"Was. A long time ago—fifteen, sixteen years. Car accident."

My eyes widened, and I let out a soft, "Oh."

"Bruce never talks about it, but after that, Emma says Bruce pretty much shut down," Stephanie explained. "His wife left. The park kind of went downhill. Not that it's dead, but it's not what it used to be." She gestured toward the wall of photos. Now that she mentioned it, I did notice—in all the black-and-white pictures from way back, there were about thirty girls. Recent years only had ten or so. This year, there were just seven. And the newspaper clippings, the last one was from the eighties.

"God," I said, thinking, *I read him so wrong.*

"He's not such a bad guy," she said. "I like Bruce. And he likes us. The mermaids, the park—it's what he's got left. I don't know what I'd do if someone that close to me died."

I knew she was thinking of her brother, so I made myself ask the question that had been weighing on my mind, just so I could stop thinking about it.

"Steven's okay, right?"

She looked at me, head tilted questioningly. "Of course he's okay. Why?"

"Nothing," I said, suddenly realizing how stupid I sounded.

"Tell me," she said.

"I'm sorry—it was stupid. I thought I heard there was something wrong with him." I found my hands up in front of me, defensive.

"Wrong, as in . . . ?" Stephanie just let the question hang there.

Finally, I finished it. "Like, mentally."

Stephanie blinked slowly, thinking, choosing her words.

"Sorry," I said, trying to head off her anger. I turned back to the wall and started looking at the pictures again, needing to look busy.

"He's autistic," she said.

My face heated instantly. I wished I could rewind my life two minutes and not bring this up at all. Lynne was right—I was like a bull in a china shop sometimes. How could I just blurt that out?

From behind me, I heard her voice, calm. "The worst part is that he's freaked out by new stuff—he doesn't like new people, doesn't like any change in his routine."

I chanced a look at her and started to breathe again. She wasn't mad at all. She came to stand next to me, facing the wall of pictures.

"Other than that, I don't see much difference between him and the rest of the world." She gestured to the wall and looked at me. "We'd all rather be living in a fantasy world, right? That's what people come here for—the customers, us, everybody."

I couldn't help but stare at her. She'd nailed it—why I was here, even why Mel did what she did. Why Mom wore an aura of serenity, drinking coffee from her chipped mermaid mug.

"We all want a little make-believe," Stephanie said, lifting her shoulders in a delicate shrug. "If you think about it, it's just a little ironic that the people who have it are considered the weird ones."

"It's not weird," I said quietly, relieved. "I just didn't know."

Stephanie smiled. "That's because it's not a big deal."

The next night, I brought dinner home from "work" for Lynne and me. It had been a while since I'd seen her, and I didn't want her to start getting suspicious about where I was spending all my time. Since it was early, I came in the side door, avoiding the courtyard.

"Did somebody order a pizza?" I asked Lynne, lifting the box temptingly.

"Ooh, yum," she said, peeking under the lid and pulling off a slice of pepperoni. "I figured you weren't eating any of that stuff," she said. "How can you actually lose weight while working at a pizza place?"

I looked at her strangely and laughed. "Lose weight?"

"Yes, definitely," she said. Her cool hands took my shoulders and steered me over to the mirror. She was right. My face *did* look thinner, less round and baby faced, and there was a little new definition going on in my upper arms.

Behind me, Lynne reached to answer the ringing phone—her nose and eyes were just visible over my head. Was I getting taller too?

"Hey there," Lynne said into the phone. "I was just talking to your daughter about how you're going to think I'm not feeding her."

Mom. My heart sped up. My eyes got wide in the mirror.

"She just brought us pizza from the boardwalk, so let me go clog my arteries and I'll put her on the phone."

Lynne winked at me as she handed me the receiver.

"Mom?" I said.

"Amy?"

"It's me," I said. She sounded far away, on her cell phone. "Where are you?"

"Driving home from work," she said. "Are you doing okay?"

I measured my words carefully, not wanting to seem like a basket case, yet careful not to seem like I was having too good a time since I was technically down here as punishment. "Yeah, I'm okay. It's been hot lately."

"Mm-hmm," she said. "Have you made any friends?"

My eyes shot to Lynne. I wondered if she'd said anything about Dylan. *Dylan.* Just thinking his name made me uncomfortable. I pressed my lips together. "Nah, not really," I said. "I haven't had time."

Another voice from inside her car said something. Mom said, away from the receiver, "Next exit."

"Mom? Who's that?"

"Tom." She paused a silent beat. "He says hi."

"I thought you said you were coming home from work?"

"He picked me up," she said. "We're going to dinner."

"Oh," I said. She hadn't wanted to talk to me just one-on-one? I dug at the seam in the wallpaper with my thumbnail, going up and down. "Is Mel there too?"

"She is." A brief hiss of static. "You want to say hi?"

"That's okay. You're kind of breaking up anyway," I said.

"We're near the bridge."

"Oh." I didn't ask which one. Didn't care. They were together, going over a bridge, to a nice little family dinner.

"Okay, then. Call me if you need me."

"Love you." I wanted to see what she would say.

I heard a horn sound—Tom, driving. Then my mom sighed. "Me too. Bye."

When I hung up, Lynne said, "That was good timing."

I sat down at the table and looked at the tomatoey-cheesy goo, my stomach still knotted and churning from the call. "Yeah," I said, hoping it didn't sound sarcastic.

"It's a shame Dylan missed this. He was here earlier but said he had somewhere to go."

I let out the breath I'd been holding in. "He's a busy guy," I said. "I'm sure we'll run into each other."

But we didn't. Not the next day, or the day after, or for so many days that soon I forgot how long it was since I'd seen him. I was so busy with the park, though, that I really wouldn't have had time to try to smooth things out with him anyway.

The walk to work had become a routine for me, one I knew by heart: out of the motel, turn right, up to the boardwalk. Sometimes I'd stop at the saltwater taffy stand and pick up a box of candy for work, for everybody to share. I'd buy extra peanut butter ones for

Bruce since those were the ones I'd watched him fish through the box for—the frown a little less deep on his face when he actually found one. Then a straight twenty-minute walk up to the end of the boardwalk, where I'd veer off, wander through neighborhoods, cross the highway, and finish the last quarter mile to the entrance. Later that day, if you asked me to recall crossing the highway, I'd have to say, "Well, I'm here—I must've crossed it." But I didn't actually remember crossing it—the same way, back at home, I'd be so used to going to school every day that sometimes I'd find myself wondering during first period if I'd locked the front door when I'd left the house.

That morning, though, I knew I'd remember crossing the highway because right afterward, an ambulance whizzed past me and turned into the entrance to Mermaid Park. And I started running like I never knew I could run before.

Paramedics were carrying the stretcher up the bleachers when I got there. Deena was on it, shaking, wet, holding an oxygen mask to her face. Her blue eyes were big, petrified.

Everyone surged up the bleachers behind her.

"You're going to be fine." Emma had a hand on the stretcher. "I'm coming along. I think you just bruised a lung."

Just bruised a lung? I looked for Stephanie, saw her down by the tank. When I got down there, I blurted, "What happened?"

Stephanie started, then stopped. Started again. "She waited too long to go for a breath. She was showing off." She turned and looked into the tank, upward, wet hair sending streams down her back and arms.

I followed her gaze. To me, the water looked so fresh, healthy. But I knew its power—except for the eel, it had kept me above the eight-foot mark for the entire summer.

"When you wait too long in there, your body starts to panic because you're running out of air." She must have seen me retract, scared to think I'd been so close to that. My stomach knotted. It could've been me.

Stephanie turned to face me. Softened a little. "This is safe if you do it right, if you respect the hugeness of all this water on top of you. Deena was showing off—when she finally bit on the hose to open the airflow, she panicked. She bit too hard. That made the air burst out like an explosion. Not that bad, but enough to bruise a lung. I think it scared her more than anything."

"She'll be okay?"

"Yeah, I mean, I did it before—once. Three years ago. I had a sharp, stabbing pain every time I inhaled for two weeks. Won't ever be that stupid again. She won't either."

"You sound so sure," I said.

Stephanie shrugged. "I can tell she won't be back."

"Who will do her shows?" I wanted to take the question back as soon as I'd asked it.

"That's up to Emma. If I had to guess?"

I shrugged.

"Ally has been training; they'll probably move her into Deena's spot. That leaves Ally's spot open."

My voice was quiet. "Where are you going with this?"

"You know where. Scared?"

"Terrified," I said. I sat down on the bleachers and brought my knees up to my chest. I rested my forehead on them. The look on Deena's face was right there when I closed my eyes. I knew that kind of fear. I felt it every night when I tried to find those air hoses.

Stephanie sat down next to me. "Look, what do I know—it's not even up to me. And besides, it's just at the top of the pool. Dropping the snowflakes during the 'Christmas in July' segment. Swimming back and forth with the cutouts of goldfish and sea horses—the ones on the long sticks. The audience won't even see you. No air hoses. No underwater stuff."

"Your timing sucks," I said down into my knees. "I would've given my right arm for this yesterday."

"Let's see what happens. If you want, I'll stay after with you tonight and practice."

I sighed. I knew if Emma came and asked me, I would do it because it meant that she and Bruce had discussed it and that he'd okayed it. I really couldn't let him down by not taking the part.

And besides, it was what I'd come here for in the first place.

It was one of those nights when you could see thousands of stars. A sliver of moon, yellowish, hung down by the horizon. This was the first time I'd been in the tank with all the lights on inside. My reflection treaded water—who knew the inside of the tank became mirrored in the brightness?

I felt like it was technically my first *legal* time in the tank. Emma had asked me earlier if I'd take over Ally's spot, and I'd shrugged and said, "I guess so." She had laughed, walking away— I didn't think I'd fooled her. She could tell I was excited.

Stephanie surfaced, an armful of weighted plastic snowflakes looped over her forearm. These I would drop, one by one, from random points on top of the tank during the Christmas medley. I'd seen it in action—the audience would laugh good-naturedly; they always did. It was the closest thing Mermaid Park had to special effects.

The second part of the job, I'd underestimated. There were six poles, each ten feet long, with some kind of sea creature on the bottom—a painted wooden cutout of a school of fish, an octopus. During the show, the audience would see them casually swimming from side to side in the background. What the audience didn't know was that there was a swimmer above pulling that fish or octopus along, swimming one-armed across the back arc of the tank. What I hadn't known until then was how heavy, really heavy, the poles were. Swimming one-armed with them along the curved surface of the tank for the duration of three practice songs, threatening to get sucked under, had me completely exhausted.

Stephanie heaved the armful of snowflakes onto the deck. Grabbed the edge and lifted herself out of the water. Not even winded.

I made my way to the edge. Hid it as I caught my breath.

"So, you got it?" she said.

"I think so."

"Want to run through it again? We can if you want."

"Nah, I think I get it." I hooked my feet over the edge and lay back on the surface of the water, looking up at the sky.

She hopped into the water. "Want to learn a trick?"

"Sure."

"Here, watch it all in action first," she said. She swam to the side of the tank, dunked, and pushed off the side. Mid-tank, she curled up into a tight ball for a flip; then she stretched herself out in a back bend, arching into an O shape suddenly for three lazy loops. When she stopped looping, she lay back flat, like she was fast asleep, and started to sink to the bottom. The overall effect made me think of an ice skater's tight turns and final sleek glide. Sadder, though, somehow.

She started kicking for the top.

"I've never seen that before," I said.

She smiled. "So, you know a basic flip."

I said, "Yeah, but there is no way I can do that whole trick."

"I'm breaking it down for you," she said. "Just follow." She demonstrated the flip. That much I knew—it was the same tight turn I used in swim meets. So far, so good. "Got it?" she said.

"Yeah." I dragged it out so she could hear the doubt in there.

"Okay, then you just snap back into a back bend underwater."

"Sounds painful," I said.

"Try it before you complain. No gravity. Makes it easier." She gestured to the side of the pool where she'd started.

I paddled over, dunked, shot out to the middle of the pool. Then did a tight flip and snap—arched into a back bend. The momentum of the whole move made me turn in two lazy Os. My fingertips, extended above and behind me, even grazed my toes. When the movement stopped, I surfaced.

Stephanie was silent for a second.

"What?" I said, suddenly self-conscious.

"Nothing. That was just good. Very good."

I gulped air, surprised.

"Now for the last part, going from the back bend to facing inward. This is what loses people. Try it first," she said.

I pushed off again, tight flip, then stretched back into an O. Then I tried to turn in to make an O shape but *facing* my knees this time. I couldn't. My body wanted to straighten out and stop awkwardly. I came to the top.

"Yeah, that's what people always do," she said. "Now try it this way: when you want to do the inward O, turn your hips first. The rest of your body will just follow without thinking."

I wanted to explain to her that the human body had this little thing called a spine and that it likes to bend a certain way, but Stephanie wasn't in a listening mood.

"Go," she ordered. "Remember, hips first."

Dunk, launch—flip, then back bend for three Os—my body knew that much and did it smoothly. Now hips, turn—there they went. My legs followed, then my torso spun last.

Wow, it had worked.

I came to a stop, looking at my kneecaps. Shocked, I did what came next—unfolded to lie back flat and let the fall begin.

My eyes open, I could see Stephanie watching me from above, her hair fanned out, skin alabaster like mine in the bright white of the tank lights.

The air in my lungs, I realized with a jolt, was gone.

I grabbed at the water around me, kicking and shoving my way up.

In the mirrored glass, I caught a glance of myself. Ghostlike, white on white in the water, all red lips and dark hair. Eyes filled with pure panic. I coughed and gasped in the air at the surface, couldn't fill up my lungs fast enough, greedy for more.

As the water drained from my ears and the pounding of my heart slowed down, I heard this sharp, rhythmic sound and had no idea what it was. I looked at Stephanie to ask her, "Do you hear that? What is that noise?"

And that's when I realized what it was.

It was her, beside me.

She was clapping.

 CHAPTER Fourteen

WHEN I GOT TO THE PARK THE NEXT DAY, I SAW THE LINEUP ON THE dry-erase board backstage in Emma's no-nonsense capital letters—

ACT I: CINDERELLA BALL

STEPHANIE, HEATHER, CARRIE, MARIA

ACT II: DISNEY TRIBUTE

ALL

ACT III: CHRISTMAS IN JULY

STEPHANIE, ALLY, CARRIE

ACT IV: PIRATES AHOY

STEPHANIE, HEATHER, MARIA

(PROPS: AMY)

I was on the board—granted, in parentheses, but my name was still there. I felt a secret thrill, remembering the first time I'd seen that board, how I'd wondered what it would feel like to glimpse my own name up there. Now I knew. Just thinking about that gave me another shiver of excitement.

I'd already put on my bathing suit at home, and ten minutes before showtime, I was up on the deck, getting all my prop fish sticks lined up, my snowflakes in a neat stack. Doing stretches to warm up, to burn off the nerves that were making me jumpy. Over the fence, I peeked at the control room, where Bruce always sat. There he was, looking at me. I gave him a wave and a thumbs-up, and he tipped his grimy baseball cap at me.

I felt like dancing, I was so happy.

There was the music cue—lots of harps and flutes. I slid into the water, knowing that down twenty feet, the mermaids were coming magically into view from below. Wondering how many people there were in the audience today.

I grabbed the first pole—the octopus. Stood it up vertically above me, slid it in octopus first along the side of the tank. Holding on to the handle with my right hand, I did a slow side-stroke across the pool. The audience would see a cute, big-eyed purple octopus making a happy sideways jaunt across the tank. Then, when I reached the side, I slid the pole up, up out of the water onto the deck. Grabbed another stick—which one was this? The flounder. Raised it up above me, slid it in alongside the tank, out of the audience's view. I was pretty warmed up. Using my left hand this time, I went with a slightly faster side-stroke. Tried to give the fishy a little up-and-down motion as I swam along.

Next. Which was this? The crab—cute. I said, "C'mon, crabby, let's go to the other side."

Three laps later, that was about when I started to wonder, why were these sticks so heavy? They felt about twenty pounds each, deadweight, trying to pull me down.

After fifteen laps, my hands were starting to cramp. I'd never noticed how long the Cinderella ball scene was, but now we were headed into the Disney tribute. I started doing a slower side-stroke, wondering if the audience noticed that the octopus had lost a little of its get-up-and-go.

Christmas in July—that number called for white snowflakes to fall from the sky down past the mermaids, who were bundled up in cute mittens and earmuffs, trimmed in white puffy stuff, like clouds. These I plunked in, every ten seconds or so, from the side of the tank. Stephanie had said I should swim around and drop them, but this was the same effect, less swimming.

My arms felt heavy. Palms red, a redder dot at the base of each finger—calluses forming.

The last number was up-tempo, quick, silly. To keep up with the beat, I was doing a half breaststroke, giving the fishies and octopus a jittery little dance, which threatened to pull my arm right out of the shoulder socket.

People would notice this, I was sure—they would see some-thing new about the show. They would want to know, who was the new girl on the fish sticks?

My breathing was heavy—as heavy as my legs felt from all the kicking.

Finally, there they were—the ending notes of the song. I knew that down below me, the mermaids were disappearing one by one through the chute.

My cue to make the fish gone. I swam to the side fast and hoisted the stick onto the deck. That was it. My first show—I'd done it.

I looked to the sky, waiting for the sound of applause. There it was.

Quiet applause.

Oh God—they hadn't liked it. Was it something I'd done wrong?

I lifted myself out onto the deck, my arms shaky and tired. I walked over to the edge of the tank-top fence and peered over.

Three people in the audience.

Three freaking people.

I plopped down on the deck, listening to the pounding of my heart. Knowing my face was too red to go down there, whether it was from the strain or the disappointment.

Heather, the complainer, had told Emma she got bonked on the head by my falling snowflakes, so I had to start swimming around to drop one in here, one in there. After a week, I'd learned to stack a bunch of them on one arm and release them gently down the front of the tank with a little twirl—that way they'd steer clear of the mermaids and give the audience the best show.

And after the calluses hardened a little, I found that holding the poles wasn't so bad. During the pirate song, I would even take one in each hand and float on my back to give it that silly, campy feel.

If anyone down below noticed, they never mentioned it. Nobody ever said anything. No, *Great job, Amy.* Or even, *Thanks for not killing me with those snowflakes, Amy.* I started to wonder what Mom would say or even Mel—if they'd get it, if they'd notice the work I was putting in that everybody else was missing.

What I wouldn't give to have someone notice. It crossed my mind that Dylan probably would have noticed if he'd been around. I'd barely seen him lately. He must have started cleaning up at the park at times when I wasn't there, and the most I caught of him at Lynne's place was his back when I was walking by.

Anyway, it was really just me up there at the top of the pool, entertaining myself. Technically part of the mermaid show, yes— but just starting to realize the truth: there was an ocean of difference between the top of the pool and everything underneath. And crossing that distance was something I knew I didn't have in me.

I was tired. Working three shows a day, I hadn't expected it to be so tiring.

Swimming back and forth up there, I dreamt of taking a break, maybe a week, to lounge at the beach—the coconut-sweet lotion making my skin all mirrored.

I dreamt of sharing a paper cone of boardwalk fries with a guy, a guy perfect like I'd thought Dylan was at first—before he turned clingy, before I saw all the stuff that was really wrong about him. I dreamt of this perfect guy who would let me put eighteen packets of ketchup all over our fries, messy, like I really liked things. Then he could run away with them down the boardwalk, making me chase him, catch him—making me work for it. Then we'd feed each other and the birds.

Stephanie and I went to the boardwalk one night after the late show. When we came to the softball booth, I felt my posture straighten, my stomach suck in—my body did it itself, without instructions.

It was like something inside me knew he was there—the gorgeous guy who worked at the booth on the boardwalk, next to the lemonade stand. The softball booth guy.

Dark eyes, intense, caught us as we walked by. My legs felt suddenly clumsy. He was watching us. I knew because I'd been watching him from the corner of my eye.

I guessed when you were used to girls stopping and taking interest, what made you *really* interested was when they blew you off. He was that kind of guy. He stood with one foot up on the counter, gripping two softballs in his right hand. He was smiling already, face right on us, knowing we'd turn and stop like girls always did when they passed guys like him.

We didn't.

So he called to our backs, "Ladies! Free throw?"

My half pause made Stephanie pause. It was late, after ten, and we were just wandering, too hot to go home.

"We can if you want," she said.

"Whatever you want," I said, not looking.

She laughed. "Come on."

We missed the first three shots and the second three shots too. When the next ball bounced back over the railing and out to the crowded boardwalk, Stephanie and I were done, laughing too hard, and the guys—Curt, the cute one, and the other guy, Mike—were laughing too.

I was folded in without question. That was nice.

"Here—you just need to arc it differently," Curt said. He hopped over the counter and stood behind me, his left hand on the waist of my gauzy cotton top. Stephanie sat on the counter, braiding a strand of her hair while Mike told a story. Seeing me looking, she smiled.

I turned my profile to Curt, not making eye contact. "You're assuming I have any control over the arc? Or that I even know what an arc is?"

"Just let go of it a little earlier," he said. His thumb found its way to the small of my back, making me feel tiny. "Throw."

I swung my arm underhand, but his hand had me so distracted, I didn't let go of the ball at all. Stephanie laughed so hard, I could see every single one of her teeth.

"So you know you have to let go, right?" Curt said.

"Maybe we should stick to the swimming, Amy," Stephanie said, wiping the tears from under her eyes.

"Oh, that's cool," Curt said. "I didn't know you worked at Mermaid Park." I could hear it—he was impressed.

I turned to face him, standing right there behind me. I took his other hand and put the softball in it. His eyes shone with my boldness.

Later, when they closed the booth, we walked up the deserted boardwalk two by two, Curt still with his hand on my back.

As we passed a streetlight, I glanced up—at his olive skin, strong chin. He looked older than the guys who were ever interested in me. Black hair, short on the sides and tousled on top, just the kind you want to touch and play with.

I couldn't believe that I was walking with this guy, that he wanted to be here with me.

My palms were sweaty. I could feel the dampness at the small of my back behind my neck. Nerves and heat too. I felt like I should say something.

"So what's your family like?"

He laughed. "A pain."

I laughed too. New topic. "How'd you end up getting this job? Do you like it?"

"It's all right. Outside, good money."

I waited for him to ask me about anything. Nothing. "So how do you guys know Stephanie?"

"I see her all the time walking by. It's a small town. We all know each other sooner or later."

"Yeah, I know what you mean."

The breeze picked up off the ocean and my hair blew like crazy. He laughed, helped me gather up the strands that were stuck to my neck. Then he held it gathered loosely, a ticklish spot. I shivered with a chill.

Up close, he smelled like soap and something sweet, tropical.

"This is a lot of hair," he said lightly.

I pointed up, caught for a moment by the whiteness of his smile. I said, "You should talk," and did what I'd wanted to do all night, touched his soft pouf of hair, his warm face, strong jaw.

I saw him bend down toward me, and I closed my eyes.

When we kissed, his mouth was open, so I opened mine too, surprised—and I guess flattered.

I crept my hands up his shoulders, around his neck. The sound of his breathing got faster.

His hands moved from the small of my back to my sides. We stepped into a little alcove by a T-shirt shop, out of view, and I tried not to stiffen as it hit me that his hands were about to start exploring up the front of my shirt.

He kissed my neck and breathed into my ear. He knew what he was doing—I could tell I wasn't the first girl these moves had been tried on. My eyes scanned the T-shirts in the window— REHAB IS FOR QUITTERS; VERY FUNNY, SCOTTY, NOW BEAM DOWN MY CLOTHES.

I tried to plug back in, moved my hands down his arms. His breathing in my ear, it was fine. Stuff like this never happened to girls like me.

I had a thought. If I asked him right now, would he remember my name?

I buried my face in his neck, trying not to laugh when I read, I'M CLEOPATRA, QUEEN OF DENIAL.

Anyway. He'd probably be winding down soon.

Rain. Three days straight of epic, cats-and-dogs rain. It kept the park closed and kept me stuck at Lynne's, telling her the restaurant had sent me home since there were no customers willing to brave the storm and wander on the boardwalk.

The steamy air smelled like something burnt, maybe ozone. I was hot, damp, sticky. The last twenty-four hours had been crackling with thunder and lightning. Lynne's neighbor's TV set had caught on fire when lightning struck the antenna. After the fire trucks left, I stayed far from the TV in Lynne's living room.

Yesterday, stir-crazy, Lynne and I had walked up to the boardwalk just to get out. The rain came at us sideways, little needles of it. Our backs to it, that left us facing the softball booth in the distance— Mike, solo, drenched, pretended to toss me a ball. I laughed.

Lynne said, "You know him?"

"Kind of. Not really. Friend of a friend." I could hear the rain loud on my hood.

Today, we'd played every board game in Lynne's collection— Scrabble, Yahtzee, Sorry, Clue. That was when boredom started to make noises in the back of my head. Mermaid Park had been closed for three days, and I needed to get out.

The moment the rain slowed, I slipped back into my windbreaker and went north.

By the time I got there, the rain had lightened to a mist. The thunder was gone, and the crickets were starting their first songs. The forest floor on either side of the driveway had flooded from the storm—when the ocean got rough, the streams would overfill and flow like mad, filled to the tippy top, pulling sod from the banks, baring trees' roots.

Inside, the storm had left the amphitheater a mess of leaves and branches. Rich, clay-colored mud had seeped in through one low holding wall; the lowest bleachers were coated in the stuff. The whole place smelled so green and alive.

And suddenly what I wanted more than anything was to get up top, to get in.

I left my windbreaker on the deck. Stepped out of my wet, muddy sneakers, one, two, then dove in headfirst, crossing the length of the pool in a single breath. Icy and clean, the water reflected the steely storm clouds above.

Droplets of rain dotted the surface. It was raining harder again. Somewhere, I heard a rumble of thunder.

When I looked up, I almost let out a surprised cry but instead just stared in shock.

Dylan was there, in his red sweatshirt with a wet hood and his swim trunks. Looking surprised to see me or doing a good job of faking it. Then in a moment, the surprise turned to something else. An expression I recognized, deep inside . . . something I'd felt on my own face.

Right after that day back at school when swim team Brian made it clear he had no idea who I was.

"I'm just here to check on the tank," Dylan said, going to the side and looking in.

I wanted to disappear, to shrink up into a single molecule, then just vanish into thin air. He was right to hate me—hate I could've taken. But I didn't expect to feel my throat close up a little with sadness when I saw that he was still hurt after all this time. God, how could I have been so mean? My head felt like it was shrinking down on my shoulders.

I tried to ease the tension a little. My voice came out too high, nervous. "That's okay. I'm probably not supposed to be here anyway," I said.

The thought hit me—he had been avoiding me too.

Quietly, I said, "How are you?"

"Fine," he said. I could see him soften a little, hearing that I was just as nervous. His broad shoulders loosened, and he shrugged. "Good, you know." Then he added, "How about you?"

My breath eased a little. At least he wasn't going to make this one of those awkward, post-hookup moments. "If I played one more game of Scrabble, I was going to go crazy. That's C-R-A-Z-Y," I spelled out. "And did you know a z is worth ten points? Lynne creamed me."

He laughed but didn't want to, I could tell.

"I hear you got into the show," he said, looking down. He'd grabbed the long-handled brush and was pushing it down the sides of the tank.

I shrugged and didn't know what to say so went for the truth. "Not really. I'm just paddling around up here."

"But that's how they train people," he said. "It doesn't happen overnight."

"I have a little problem with the whole air hose thing," I said, looking up at the clouds. It actually felt good to say it, to get it out there.

"Because of what happened to Deena?"

A roll of my eyes. "Goes way farther back. It's just how far down they are." I gestured at the millions of gallons of water below me. "I can swim like a fish. I just can't breathe underwater like one."

"Wait, is it the air hoses or the deep that freaks you out?"

"You mean, which one's worse? I guess the deep part."

"Really?" Looking at me now. "But you're an amazing swimmer, Amy."

I turned my head a little so he could only see my profile. "It just feels weird," I said. "The pressure. Did I ever tell you I was born two months early?"

"No."

"I was. I was early and my body hadn't developed all the way—heart, lungs."

"I didn't know that. But anyway, you're fine now. Right?"

"Yeah, I guess."

He breathed out, looked somewhere far away. The raindrops deadened all the sound, the crickets, the birds. It was just me and him and a hundred thousand tiny drops dripping into this pool on top of a spring spurting out of the ground. Where water from the sky met water from the earth and mixed into something else completely.

He slipped off his sweatshirt, kicked off his shoes. Lowered himself to the edge and motioned me over. My breath held in my chest, I treaded closer.

He wiped the rain from his nose, slicked his hair back with one hand—it stood back, like he was going through a strong wind. I licked my lips, wondering. He pointed down to my legs—past my legs, actually, to the hose by the grid, where Stephanie had let the eel out.

"That's the top air hose in the pool," he said, locking eyes with me, all business. I nodded. "That's at twelve feet. They go every six feet from there, down to the bottom, which is thirty-six feet."

My eyes widened—thirty-six feet?

"Look, even if you were at the bottom and panicked and you shot up to the top, you'd still be okay. You only need to stop and decompress if you go below forty feet, which you don't."

I laughed. "You're right—*I* won't."

"Ten feet, twenty feet, thirty feet—it's all the same as long as you have air," he said. "You think you'll pop or something?" A smile.

I didn't smile back. This wasn't stupid.

"Look, it's in your head." A few hairs had started to fall forward again, wet. "Prove it. Come down to the first hose with me."

"Right."

He slid into the water next to me. Serious eyes, challenging me. Reminding me of that kid in the pool earlier this summer. "I'll go first and wait for you," he said, already looking down. "Remember, bite gently on the hose—it opens the seal and air will come into your mouth. Breathe in through your mouth. Stop biting when you have enough air." He took a deep breath, and suddenly he was gone.

I watched him make his way down, strong arm muscles crossing the distance in a few thrusts. He found the hose, breathed in. Looked up at me, still at the top.

Then the hand gesture from him—come down here.

I waited. He did it again.

I gestured back, come on up. I had to laugh—he was cute, trying.

I waited, but he didn't move. Every once in a while, he'd draw a breath from the hose, and I'd see a new, silvery trail of bubbles work their way up. They'd break at the surface, right beside me.

I looked back down. His eyes were on me, the challenge there.

He would wait, I was realizing. How he could always bring out the side of me that wanted to push back, I didn't understand.

That was my last thought as I dunked under and thrust my feet upward, a counterweight, headed straight down, down, down the back of the tank. It was like the white underbelly of a whale, endless and cold.

My eardrums squeaked in protest as water tried to push its way in.

Heading straight down, bubbles streamed out of my nose up into my swimsuit.

Down below me, Dylan looked up—his hair a cloud of silk around his head. Hand outstretched. I reached for him.

In his hand was the hose. My fingers found the vent in the wall, which had been swung open from the rushing water of the rain. It was something to grip to keep me here. I moved the hose to my lips between my teeth, the gentlest of bites.

And nothing.

My heart stopped right then. I dropped the hose, eyed the top of the tank—it stretched too far away. Dylan saw it. He grabbed my shoulders and shook his head slowly at me.

He gestured biting, a swift, harder move. Then he put the hose to my lips again.

I bit. This time, I felt a gradual hiss of air, cool and normal. I breathed in until I was full. The relief washed over me. I smiled at him, big, ready to burst, and handed him the hose back.

He smiled back and breathed, and as I turned to head for the top, I felt him touch my elbow.

Stay, he gestured. He offered me the hose again.

So I did. He kept his eyes locked on me, cautious. With each breath, I got a little more comfortable. It was like breathing through a snorkel, constricted but definitely air.

Floating there, in suspension, we watched each other breathe. My heart came back to its normal pace. Those light eyes were locked on me, concerned. Silver air bubbles of the tiniest size were caught in his eyelashes, not letting go.

His eyes lit up suddenly—pure delight, looking over my shoulder. I turned to follow his gaze.

From the overflow tunnel, the tentative nose of a creature. Marble gray, with dark eyes shiny like river rocks. Slowly, it emerged the rest of the way into the tank.

Plump, rounded body with small hand-like flippers. A fan-shaped tail.

I couldn't believe my eyes.

It was a manatee.

A little one—not even half the size of an adult—had gotten flushed into the stream during the storm. It must have thought the overflow chute was a way out.

Dylan and I froze, holding tight to the vent. After a moment, he held the hose to me. I took a breath, passed it back.

The manatee looked our way, surprised. Graceful and strong, it swung itself around with a quick swish of its tail to look at us head-on.

I saw Dylan raise a hand and move it back and forth. Waving.

The manatee liked it. Rolled a lazy flip, came closer.

It came up to my face and let a few silvery air bubbles out of its nose. The expression was so human, I laughed. My hand reached up slowly to touch its thick gray skin, sliding along the warm smoothness. If my eyes had been closed, I would've guessed I was touching another human.

I'd seen manatees before in books—Mom's mermaid books, which said sailors would mistake manatees sunning themselves on coastal rocks for women who lived in the sea. That was how the legend of mermaids was born, or at least that's what some people said.

I glanced at Dylan; he looked back and smiled.

And when we looked back, the manatee was gone—just the tip of her tail visible down the chute, headed back to the ocean to sun on rocks where she would make men tell fantastical stories, tall tales, of places that maybe did exist undersea.

Dylan slid the vent into place, covering the opening. We each took a final breath from the hose and headed to the surface.

The rain had stopped for the first time in three days. The crickets were back, the mossy smell of the forest reaching through again. We pulled ourselves onto the edge of the tank, our feet still in the water.

Finally, I said, "That wasn't so hard."

On the way out, up the bleachers, Dylan said he wanted to check for flooding in the cellar.

"Cellar?"

"Well, it's not really a cellar," he said. "It's the maintenance area. Over there." He pointed to the set of metal double doors I'd almost gone into once, the ones I'd thought led to the supply room.

Dylan climbed the bleachers, loped onto the slippery grass hill. One hand lifted each handle, and suddenly there was a hole in the ground. As I peered over his shoulder, I could see the first three rungs of a rusted metal ladder before the pitch black swallowed it.

A flashlight was hooked on the first rung. Clever.

Dylan flicked it on. A weak yellow light revealed ten more ladder rungs, a dirt floor the color of sunset, reds, oranges. Moist but not flooded.

"Good," he said.

"What's down there?"

"Just plumbing." Flashlight off, doors closing. "Tools. Nobody uses it."

"Learning all kinds of new things today," I said.

"Imagine that," he said. "And I bet you thought you knew it all."

My mouth tightened. I avoided his eyes. He looked at me until I had no choice but to look up.

"Come on. You deserved that." I could tell he felt bad—to him, stinging people like that didn't come naturally.

In the back of my head, Stephanie's voice: *Defrost.*

So I let his self-conscious grin make me smile. "Yeah, I guess you owed me one."

He offered me a ride back to the motel on his mountain bike, even though I already had "ride double on a bike" crossed off my list of things to do in life. This time, I clamped my hands around the T-bar to hold on.

At the foot of the driveway, Bruce's truck was pulling in. Dylan biked up to his window and held on to the mirror for balance.

"Hey, Bruce," Dylan said. "Nothing flooded this time."

"Good," he said. Then to me, "You checking up on things?" He sounded amused. Maybe he liked that I would worry about this place even when I wasn't on the clock.

"Yep," I said, a smile pulling at my cheeks till I thought they would keep me from being able to talk right. "Everything is under control, Captain."

Bruce laughed—a rare sound—before continuing his way down the bumpy road toward the park.

Stephanie and I were killing time before the two-thirty show. "Hey, wanna see this cool drawing Steven sent me?" She brought a letter out of her backpack and held it up so I could see what he'd drawn on the paper. The lines took on shape, three-dimensionality, before my eyes. A stone stairway, steep, viewed from the top.

"Bring it closer," I said, still at the edge of the pool, my hands too wet to hold it. Up close, I could see that the attention to detail was painstaking. Every shadow was a patch of fine, cross-hatched lines. It was amazing.

"He's the most focused person I know," she said. "When we were little, he could just sit in his room and draw for hours and hours."

I pushed off the wall, started treading water. "So what comes after the triple loop?"

"You won't like it," she said, folding up the drawing, tucking it away in a plastic bag.

"Why?"

"It involves air hoses."

"Try me," I said.

She stopped, looked at me. Hands went to her slim hips, chin dipped low in shock. "Try me?"

"Try me!" I shouted, louder, with a smile.

She was already coming in before I could change my mind, and just before the splash, I heard her say, "Where did the real Amy go?"

I dunked under and followed her.

I'd gotten into a rhythm with the shows, always adding a little something different each time. That day's performance, I swam back and forth, one pole in each arm, making the mom fish and the little school of guppies travel together. Nibble playfully at the fake kelp forest. Play hide-and-seek with each other. Little games like this, it was how I passed the day.

When the song ended, I made them take a bow, then swam to the side and slid them out. That's when I saw Emma's sensible Ecco clogs, standing right there at the edge. She'd been watching me.

My first thought was, *Oh God, I'm in trouble.*

"Hi," I said. I used one hand to shield my eyes from the sun. It was too bright to read her look. "Is everything okay?"

Finally, "Amy, aren't we becoming quite the swimmer?" she said.

My squint turned into a smile. It was weird, not seeing her expression—was this sarcasm? I decided to take it at face value.

"Thanks, Emma. I guess we are."

Her silhouette shook its head. Was that a chuckle? "We're always the smart-ass too. It's lucky I like you."

Stephanie and I were both floating on our backs at the top of the tank. Near each other—near enough to talk, even with our ears underwater.

"Why don't you come back next summer?" Stephanie said.

"Maybe," I said. My voice sounded muffled, far away inside my head.

"Come," she said.

"There's still a week left to *this* summer," I said. "Besides, it's complicated. It's not just about what I want."

"Your mom wants you to be happy."

"Maybe, when she thinks about it."

"Hmm."

"That came out worse than I meant. She's just unhelpful. Neutral. Switzerland. So caught up in herself she forgets to look at the rest of the world."

Stephanie swished her arms to come closer. She was just above my head. "What does she say when you tell her that?"

"I shouldn't have to tell her."

"You aren't afraid to tell Tom to go to hell."

My turn to be quiet. "Well, he should."

"Oh. And if you tell your mom to go to hell, she might. She might be done."

How could Stephanie always do that? Just say it plain like that. My throat had a hard time swallowing. Still, I said, "Before she met him, it was the three of us. Me and Mel and her. She knew me then. Like she knew herself."

"You changed too, though. Mel too. People do. It can be good again but different."

My laugh came out like a cough. My eyes were wet. She was right—we'd all changed. Who was it who'd said that creatures had to change to survive? Was it Darwin?

"Maybe one day I can go to the same college as you," I said. I liked the idea of it—the two of us making ramen noodles in a hot pot, watching *Three's Company* reruns.

"And Steven can be at a school nearby," she said, sounding far away.

I floated there, thinking about how Stephanie loved her brother, more than I understood. I laid my head back down on the water and heard my ears fill with water, the sound rushing like an approaching wave. It was something our siblings had in common—each of them had fault lines deep to their core.

I was down to the fourth air hose in the back of the tank. That put me at thirty feet, the deepest I'd been. I'd been gradually working my way lower and lower, and today I didn't want to go back up to the surface. The pressing weight of all that water on my body was actually feeling good. Really good. Strengthening.

I took a breath, pushed off the back wall, and swam to the front wall. Then another spin, push off, and I came back for another breath.

Stephanie had shown me the last move in the end-of-summer solo she was practicing—a series of diagonal loops, bottom left to upper right, then bottom right to upper left.

A three-dimensional figure eight.

The effect of a coin spinning on its edge, slowing down, stopping.

And then there was the ending—this was the only performance where the mermaid didn't exit through the tube in the bottom.

"I just sort of rise up, arms extended, all the way out of their view," Stephanie said.

"It just ends like that?"

"The idea is, the Mermaid Queen rises to the sky and stays there till next summer," she said.

I rolled my eyes way up to the sky and sighed.

"What?"

"It's just a little . . . hokey."

She flicked water at me. "Hokier than Cinderella? Who, I might add, can't even wear a glass slipper because she has fins?"

"That's true."

"It's pretty. You'll see."

Down deeper, practicing after Stephanie left, I took a few relaxed breaths through the hose, then pushed off the wall for another lap. As I neared the glass, there was a face looking in.

Looking right at me, hands splayed on glass.

Through the water, fuzzy, pixie-cut graying hair, a woman's broad shoulders.

I got close enough to see features.

Lynne.

The shock on her face was visible; color drained from her cheeks. Then she mouthed the words, *Get. Out. Of. There. Now.*

CHAPTER *Fifteen*

WE WERE IN LYNNE'S CAR, DRIVING DOWN THE ROAD AWAY FROM the park. My ears were whooshing. My blood pumped. My heart pounded.

Lynne knew.

She *knew.* She knew I'd lied. She knew I'd been here all summer, the place where she'd told me not to go.

In an instant, everything had changed. Just one more week and I would've gotten away with it. My chest ached with the weight of that thought.

Lynne's lips were white, pressed together tightly. Her breath was sharp, fast, in and out of her nose, though she drove slow and safe. "I had to find you," she said, a quick look over to me, then back to the road. "Your mother called. She can't find Melissa."

"Can't *find* her?"

"No. She left."

"She ran away?" The questions raced through my mind—*How*

long has she been gone? Where did she go? But what came out was, "How did you know where I was?"

A frown pulled the corners of her mouth down. "That was horrible, Amy. I went to every goddamn pizza place on the boardwalk. Nobody knew you. First Melissa's gone, and then I couldn't find you either." She shook her head, mad at herself and at me. "I couldn't find Dylan—your friend at the softball booth told me where you worked."

"Mike," I murmured.

"Thank God I found you. I can't believe I didn't know about this sooner. Your mother is not going to like this," she said.

I could picture Mom, her eyes big, hearing of Lynne finding me at the bottom of some giant water tank on the side of town where girls really aren't safe walking alone. She would freak out.

I snuck a glimpse over at Lynne. She was still shaking her head in disbelief. "I can't believe you were at the mermaid place. All this time. This whole goddamn summer."

I sank down in the passenger seat, holding my knees. Goose bumps raised in the AC from the dashboard vents. "So where is Mel? How long has she been gone?"

"She was gone this morning. They think she left sometime last night."

Where would she have gone? "Did they try Trina's?"

"Yes, she hadn't heard anything."

"What made her leave?"

Lynne exhaled sharply and glanced at me from the corner

of her eye. "Your mother said she'd been fighting with Tom."

"Tom," I said, like, *of course*. Wheels churned fast in my head, running through places Mel might have gone. I came up empty and was saddened by the thought that if she were in my shoes and I were missing, she'd have no idea where to find me either.

I slid onto the stool behind the counter in the motel office, still in my swimsuit, damp from the mermaid tank. My knees were shaking and my hands were too. I rested my forehead on the counter, trying to bring my breathing back to normal.

I should never have stayed down here this summer.

I'd thrown her to the sharks when I left her alone. Especially once I knew about the book and all her lies—she was in so much trouble, and I'd just left her.

Now she could be anywhere. Someone could have found her and taken her. I swallowed hard, fighting the urge to throw up as I tried not to think about the possibilities.

Mom would blame me.

We would all wish it had been me instead—all of us.

How could I have been so selfish?

I heard Lynne sigh heavily as she reclined in one of the red vinyl chairs.

She said, "So. How did you find that place?"

I lifted my chin, rested it on my forearms, trying to clear my head. I thought back to the beginning of the summer here. It seemed a lifetime ago now. "I went out walking, sort of just ended up at the park." It was out there now, weird to be talking about it.

"I told you not to go up there," she said.

I looked down. "I know. I'm sorry. It's not really bad at all, though."

"Amy, I'm not going to argue with you. I told you not to go there and you went. End of story. Thank God you didn't get hurt," she said. Her eyes closed.

"The swimming is safe once you know what you're doing," I said with certainty. She seemed to be considering that. In the back of my head, I felt a selfish little surge of hope—I might have my foot in the door to an argument on why I should keep working there. Why we didn't have to tell anyone about this. It could be our secret, mine and Lynne's.

Yes, I bet I could convince her.

Just then, there was a tap on the door. On top of the TV, the dog lifted his head, waking up but too tired to bark.

The door opened a bit, then wider. Lynne's breath drew in.

I let out a sharp gasp.

It was Mel.

I closed my eyes to clear the tears. One, two, three—I opened them again. Mel was still there, wrapped in a hug from Lynne. She looked pale and sweaty, her navy overstuffed backpack over one shoulder, sliding down her arm to the ground with a soft thud.

Her eyes shifted to me. They were red-rimmed. She'd been crying.

"Hi," I said. I stood up on shaky legs and ran to her, grabbing her tightly in a hug. Her bony shoulders felt unfamiliar in my arms. I squeezed her tight and rocked her back and forth, getting used to the feel of her again.

She didn't say anything, and I wondered if a hug from me wasn't what she'd wanted. Then soft sobs shook her, growing harder with each one.

"You're okay now," I said. I swayed back and forth with her, trying to calm her down.

"You don't know what it's like, dealing with him all by yourself," she said.

I took her by the shoulders and held her at arm's length to see if she was serious. Had she forgotten what I'd been carrying all this time? Who his favorite punching bag was? Suddenly we both noticed, Lynne had picked up the phone and was dialing.

"What are you doing?" Mel asked her.

My eyes leveled at Lynne's—worried now but for a different reason. "You don't need to do that," I said.

"I know what I need to do," Lynne said. "They'll want to know Mel is safe."

Melissa's breathing was hard, heavy. She sounded like she was about to lose it again. Lynne pulled the phone around the corner to the hallway so she could talk.

"How did you get here?" I said to Mel finally.

"Bus." A fast shake of her head. "It got worse every day. You don't even know. He just attacks and attacks." Her voice got thick in the back of her throat.

"It's always that way. For me."

"I fucking hate him." She focused on picking up her backpack. A long blink cleared the tears that were about to spill out. "Amy, he was so much worse than before," she said. "Now that he's home all day, I can't even breathe without him screaming at me."

"Yeah, welcome to my world," I said.

Another quick shake of her head. "I'm tiptoeing around the house, afraid all the time. He criticizes everything I do. He insults me—I'm stupid, I'm selfish, I'm greedy. Just one right after the other. I can't stand it. He wasn't this bad before."

"Yes, he was," I said firmly, trying to catch her eyes. She needed to understand that without me there to soak up half of it, she was getting the Tom I usually got. "Mel, this is just Tom. This is how he treats me every day. This is nothing new. You're there. You see it."

She shook her head. "He's not this bad with you, Amy. You don't know."

What? Was she really that out of touch with reality? "Mel, I *do* know," I said, trying not to lose control.

Mel let out a frustrated breath. Tears were threatening to spill over again. "Of course, how could I forget. Everything is always about you."

My hands dropped from her shoulders, letting go. Screw her. She could deal with the fallout of this on her own.

The sound of Lynne hanging up broke our conversation. "Your mom's on her way." Then to me, "She says for you to start packing too."

I spun toward her. "Me?" The look that crossed Lynne's eyes said it all. "You *told* her?" My tone was sharp, accusatory.

Lynne's gaze softened. "Of course I told her, honey."

Mel said, "Told her what?"

"I can't believe you," I said, shouting at her, surprised at how angry I was.

Lynne's mouth hung open.

"You were supposed to be on my side," I said, on the brink of losing it completely.

"This isn't about sides, Amy. This is about family. They need to know you're safe too."

That did it. I was out the door and running away, bare feet pounding on the asphalt, cutting through side streets so she couldn't find me even if she tried. Little pebbles dug into the soles of my bare feet.

People shot me worried looks as I pushed past.

I didn't feel a thing.

Someone had left the park's fence perched open a little. I slid in sideways, then saw Emma behind the ticket counter. She looked up at the noise.

My red cheeks and crazy hair, she took it all in. "You heard," she said.

I jerked back, surprised. Did she mean the Mel thing? How did she know? Confused, I said back, "*You* heard?"

She shook her head. "Stephanie just left."

"She left," I repeated, a little disappointed. "Oh, well, that's okay."

Emma looked down, figuring something. Then back at me. "No, honey, she left for her brother's."

Everything faded except two bright pinholes of light from the ticket booth. Nothing around me at all. "What? Did something happen?"

"She had to go. This happened before," she said. She leaned forward, her aging hands on the cracked wood of the counter. That was all I could look at. She saw I still wasn't getting it. "Her brother got into a fight with his new roommate—it was the third one this month. They're making him transfer somewhere else."

My hands were on the counter suddenly next to hers. Aged, smooth, aged, smooth. The pattern of our hands.

"But she's supposed to start school in two weeks."

"She'll go," Emma said. I saw her hands pressed on top of mine but couldn't feel it. "In spring, probably."

"Can't her parents do it?"

Emma shrugged. "Stephanie handles Steven better than her parents. They let her kind of run the show."

"She isn't coming back," I said. I knew it too. Two peas in a pod. She would stay there as long as he needed her, even though I needed her here.

I walked out with Emma, but once her car left the lot, I climbed back over the fence and looked for somewhere to spend the night, knowing that if he knew the whole story, Bruce really wouldn't mind. He would want me to be here.

I didn't want anyone to find me. They would have to pull me from here tomorrow kicking and screaming. Fine. That was the way it would be. First, I had to figure out where to spend the night.

Backstage would work.

I slipped into the dusty darkness of the cavernous backstage area, gliding my fingers along the dry-erase board where I knew my name was written. The thought of it being erased tomorrow when Mom dragged me home—it made my hands clench into fists. I felt my way to the steps and sat down heavily on the lowest one, letting the splinters bite into the backs of my thighs.

I'd been alone in this place so many nights, but tonight the noises were crazy, or maybe I just noticed them more. The squeaks and cracks of the building settling. The bubbling of the tank. I hugged my knees to my chest and froze, listening closely when I heard a light thump across the room. I made myself breathe—maybe it was a lost cat and not a rat, or a squirrel, or a skunk. Or a rabid raccoon. I hugged my knees tighter and risked a glance into the dark corner. Twin reflections of animal eyes stared back at me, startled.

I shot to my feet, backing out of there into the amphitheater, racing up the bleachers in giant leaps, then up the ladder to Bruce's control room

Bare plywood walls on three sides and a window on the fourth that overlooked the audience and the pool. Under the window, a homemade wooden bench held a tape deck. This was all that made up Mermaid Park's nerve center.

I ran my fingers along the table where Bruce would sit, overlooking the shows. It was sanded smooth and cool to my touch. Next to the tape deck was a black dial—I figured it was the volume, and since the tape deck was empty, I gave it a spin to test it. To my surprise, the pool lit up—I hadn't known there was a control up here too.

I spun the dial left and right, watching the light brighten and fade, brighten and fade. On my third turn, I saw them—the doors set into the hillside.

The maintenance cellar. Of course. The perfect hiding place.

I left the tank light on low and made my way downstairs.

I opened the doors, flicked on the flashlight, and took careful steps down the rusted ladder, pulling the doors closed behind me.

Sweet clay—the air was rich with the smell.

The cool ground under my feet was soothing, a little wet.

Under me, I knew, was the source of the tank's water—an artesian spring. A body of water held within layers of earth and sand and rock. It had found a way out, here at the park—crept through cracks and holes and burrowed its way through to fresh air.

I sat down against the wall, still in my bathing suit from practice earlier—I'd never had a chance to change. The cool clay clung to me, to the backs of my legs, my arms.

I flicked off the flashlight, not wanting to see or think or wonder what was going to happen to me. In less than one minute, I was asleep.

When I finally woke up, I was disoriented—no idea how long I'd been down there. Time was impossible to count or estimate. It could have been ten minutes, ten hours. I didn't know, and I was lifted a little by the thought that maybe it didn't matter.

I wondered how long I could stay down here before being found out. I felt myself smile, realizing I could probably stay down here for days or maybe longer. I might be able to stay till I couldn't take the quiet anymore.

I kicked myself, wishing I'd grabbed my toothbrush, books, a pillow. More batteries. I wished again I knew what time it was. If it was still night, I could sneak out to the snack counter and grab supplies.

I started making a list in my head.

1. Food
2. Bathroom?? Bucket/toilet paper. (Ew.)
3. Paper and pen to keep me busy
4. Batteries or a candle w/matches. Yes, a candle would be great. I could probably find batteries, a close second, in the control room over the auditorium.

By the light of the flashlight, I explored the shallow room to see what else I might already have at my fingertips.

Fat steel pipes with chunky rivets sounded empty when I

knocked on them. Hollow echoes traveled down the length of the pipes, then deadened into the wall.

Rakes, three different sizes. Shovels, both for dirt and for snow.

Thick canvas pillowcases printed with a cement mix logo. Down here, wet for years, their contents had hardened, pushed at the seams till they broke, leaving lumpy cement squares, useless in a stack, too heavy to get up the ladder. They would just stay here forever, I guessed.

I knelt down on the soft clay. Its wetness felt good on my kneecaps, down the fronts of my shins.

On the lowest shelf of a bookcase, I found a can with a pull-ring top—I took a whiff inside. Tang. There were three cans of it, all several years old but probably still drinkable. I licked my finger and dipped it in the Tang mixture. My taste buds woke up, startled by the sour sweetness.

I slid a wooden crate off the top shelf and set it softly in the clay beside me. Inside, I found a stack of papers, wrapped in a heavy sheet of waterproof canvas. The square bundle was tied gift style with a thick rope, bow on top. I untied it.

Old photos inside, a thin stack of them. It was Bruce as a young man.

He was handsome, dark-haired. Curly on top. Wide-chested with muscled arms, with his wife and a baby. Skip, I guessed. Cute together. Happy.

I stuck my finger in the Tang, then in my mouth, letting my taste buds overload on sunshiny orange.

Then Skip as a teenager. My age, tall and broad like his dad. Wild hair, long to his shoulders.

I held the picture farther away from me, trying to be objective. Yes, he was handsome for sure. Standing in front of a car—his own, you could tell from the way he sat on it. There was owner-ship in his body language.

I flipped to the next picture. It was another of Skip, a close-up taken in bright sunlight, with him looking right at the camera, bold. His squint made a furrow in his brow—vertical creases in his forehead that made him look serious.

I had seen that look a hundred times before in the mirror. I could tell from this picture, Skip was like me. A squinter and maybe a worrier, too. He wore his feelings on his face.

Deep thinking like this, this was what happened when I had too much quiet.

I looked farther up—on the topmost shelf, books. I stood, grabbed a few, and knelt back down on the ground.

Between two of the books, something slid out. Another picture. I took it between two fingernails, not wanting to get it dusty or Tangy. I glanced at it as I laid it on top of the stack.

And my heart stopped.

It was Mom. Her high school graduation picture—same as the copy in Lynne's living room. I'd seen it a hundred times.

A chill ran through me, and I grabbed the flashlight and looked around the room, sure that someone was standing there, breathing down my neck. Only the red clay walls stared back at me, old pipes, a stack of books.

I looked back at it, sure it had to be a mistake—maybe someone who just looked like her.

No, that face. I knew that face. The little doll chin. Around her neck, a thin necklace with one two three tiny pearls all in a row. It was my mother.

Maybe my grandparents had sold the book once at a yard sale a million years ago, forgetting they'd stuck Mom's picture inside for safekeeping. Or maybe Lynne's parents—that would make sense. They'd lived down here. They'd been close with Mom's parents. They'd loaned somebody this book on the beach, and Mom's picture had been inside.

I grabbed the pile of books and flipped through, looking for more photos.

As my eyes took in the next one that slipped out, my heartbeat sounded in my ears, a steady thud, heavy like footsteps.

Skip was standing behind Mom with his arms around her shoulders. She had her head tilted back, looking up at him. The hollows in her neck, graceful, younger. Her eyes half closed in delight.

He looked straight into the camera. In his body language was that same ownership. The deep lines between his brows were there and something else, deep-set eyes, a slight downturn to the corners of his mouth.

My fingers played with the picture, trying to make sense of it.

Stuck to the back of it was another picture, an underwater shot. The last bit of the Mermaid Queen choreography, the rising.

And the woman whose arms were outstretched, rising to the surface, where the queen would stay till the next summer—I knew that face.

That doll chin, that upturned nose. Tiny dots on her necklace—three pearls.

That was Mom.

I stood up with the flashlight, making myself breathe but feeling like my lungs still weren't getting air.

I looked down, focusing, to quiet the pounding in my chest. On the ground, I saw that the marks from my knees had stayed there, little scoops pushed out of the red clay.

How had my mom never mentioned this?

This hadn't been a case of forgetting. This had been hidden from me. I rushed up the ladder and burst through the double doors, gasping for air. I pulled in the cool night air, my lungs greedy for it.

And that's when I saw Mom. She was right outside. Looking for me.

CHAPTER *Sixteen*

"This whole summer," she said, her soft voice shaking. "This whole summer you were here." It wasn't a question.

I nodded. My breath was slowing. My heartbeat coming back, sort of, but still racing.

The blue light of the tank lit one side of her face. Her hair, tousled, not sleek like usual.

"What happened here?" I was surprised how calm my voice sounded. I needed her to outline it all for me—how she had gotten here. Why she'd never told me about it. Was this why she carried mermaid key chains and always wore little pearl earrings? It had been in front of me for so long.

Mom sat down on the bench—it was lower than she realized, so she plopped down hard. She looked away and slowly shook her head.

"No, what? No, you're not going to tell me how you left out this gigantic chunk of your life? Did you just happen to forget to mention it for the last sixteen years?"

"You weren't supposed to know."

"No kidding," I said, without sarcasm. "Does Dad know about him?"

Her head reared up fast. "No!" I winced. The skin around her eyes was white, tight with fear. "No one knows."

The way she said it . . . something hit me. There was something else. Something bigger.

A ringing sound came back to my ears, the thud-thud of my racing heart.

I took a step backward and shot down the ladder.

I slid across the wet floor in three long strides, slipping and feeling my legs fall out from under me. The world spun sideways, hard, and I hit the ground with my hip, my upper back.

The flashlight clacked dangerously against the bookcase but stayed lit.

Up on one elbow, I wiped the thick clay from the flashlight's lens. My hands felt around the top of the crate, grabbing the picture, bringing it to my face.

Deep-set eyes on a square face.

The dark hair, crazy with curls.

The furrow in the brow.

It was like looking in a mirror. My dirty fingers touched his image, first his eyes, then his hands, then his mouth, memorizing the features of my real father.

I tried to inhale, but my lungs were locked tight.

My heart was slamming against my chest, pounding, about to burst.

I was going to die.

My eyes closed. I didn't care.

Deep in me, a cry sprang up. It started in my gut, pushing through the layers that kept it buried. My neck arched, letting it bubble out in a scream: "Mom!"

Her footsteps came fast to the top of the ladder. "Amy!" Her feet were on the rungs, coming down fast.

Sobs heaved in my chest. Sweet air filled my lungs, and I gasped for it.

Her voice was thick and shaking. "Where are you? Give me your hand."

"Here," I said, reaching up and grabbing her hand. She knelt down fast and grabbed me, hugged my head to her chest. Her breath was hard and ragged. The flashlight made her outline big on the ceiling.

I touched her face. It was wet with tears. I cried into her shirt, "Tell me."

She sniffled wetly, breathed raspy. "Tell you what? That I lost him?" A short laugh, angry. "It wasn't fair."

Gone. My father was dead. I had never known him, and he was dead.

My hot tears wet her shirt. "You should have told me."

Her voice high and defensive, she said, "He was already gone."

"He was *my* father." I tried to pull away from her, but she held tight. She wouldn't let me go. All the frustration came out in loud, racking sobs.

I could hear her doing the same thing.

All these years, I had called the wrong person my father.

We held tightly to each other, shaking with sobs, too tired to fight any more.

When the sound of our breathing came back to normal, I had to say out loud what kept running through my mind. "So Dad doesn't know anything."

Mom was very still. Only her hands shook.

"No."

"Did anybody know? Besides you guys?"

"Lynne knew him," she said. "She loved him. She knew how much losing him broke my heart. But she didn't . . . know about you. I decided nobody should know. Nobody found out. Nobody." Almost song-like in the repeating. "When your dad came around, wanting to get back together, I just decided it was the right thing to do. I didn't know what else to do."

I pulled away from her, up on an elbow. My voice was a hoarse whisper. "Wait. Walk me through it."

"We'd broken up that summer. . . ."

"Then you met Skip," I said, connecting the dots.

"We were so in love," she said. In the glow of the flashlight, she took a fast look at me, her lips pressed together to stop the shaking. "It sounds stupid, but it was like a storybook."

"When did you find out you were going to have me?"

"I went back the first week of September, and my period was

late. I just knew. I felt so sick—I was worried about telling my parents I was moving down here, to be with him. We were going to get married." Her voice caught; she touched her chest, cleared her throat. "They had no idea. They still wanted me to get back together with your dad." She grimaced, shook her head, wondering if she should correct that.

"Keep going," I said quietly.

"All that week, he was so worried about me," she said.

"Worried?"

"About me, dealing with all that. He worried about me. About us." She pressed my leg with her own. I glanced away, trying not to cry. When I looked back, her eyes were far away and welled up with tears.

"Late one Sunday night, he made up his mind. We were on the phone and he said he was coming to get me, and I said it was crazy, driving all that way so late. But I was laughing, so happy that he was coming for me." Tears finally streamed down her cheeks. She didn't seem to notice.

"He stood you up?" I said, throwing out what I wanted the answer to be.

The corners of her mouth pulled down sharply. "I was still up waiting at five a.m. I knew something was wrong—it was a far drive, and it was Labor Day weekend, with all the traffic, but it shouldn't have taken him that long."

"He . . . crashed?"

"Coming to see me. To take me back here. *Us* back here."

A wave of nausea gripped my stomach, and I swallowed over and over till it went away. "Wait—" I said. I lifted my clay-caked fingers. "That was, what—early September?"

"Yes," barely a whisper. She was back there, remembering it all. "Last time I saw him, it was the week before Labor Day." I counted months. August, September, October, November, December, January, February, March, April, May. I was born in the middle of May.

Nine months, not seven.

Not premature.

My head reared back from her.

"I can't *believe* you." I sat up, moved away from her. "You lied about that too."

"What?" Her laugh sounded short, bitter.

"Do you know all this time, I was worried about being careful because I had been born too early. My heart? Ring a bell?" I pounded my chest with my muddy hand. My sharp yell absorbed into the thick walls around us.

"Really?" Mom said, her gentleness throwing me. "I didn't know, Amy."

I read her face for more lies. She looked back at me levelly, her chin fighting not to shake.

"I didn't know. I didn't know you thought that," she said. Her hand reached out and took both of mine, pulled me forward to know she was being straight with me. Her brows drew down serious, and she said, "You're strong, too strong sometimes." She leaned in close, so close I could smell her perfumed shampoo, the saltiness of her sweat. "There is nothing in the world wrong with you. I didn't know you thought there was."

The tears I'd been holding back, they came and came, and they wouldn't stop, not when Mom held me tight again, not even when the glow of the flashlight eventually started to wobble and fade.

It strobed in and out like a hazard sign. Slower, though.

Touching arms and knees, we both leaned back against the wall. Breathing in sync. Catching our breath, me figuring out what to do next.

It was too much, trying to process all of this at once. Too much. But then I remembered the other photo—my mother, the Mermaid Queen. "Tell me about you here," I said softly.

"That summer I lived with Lynne, we loved this place," she said.

"You swam here?"

"After a while, they let me."

"I always thought you just loved mermaids."

The flashlight ebbed, surged. I could see a shine to her eyes.

I smiled at her. I tried hard to ignore the sadness that was tugging at the corners of my mouth, making it hard to swallow. I managed a wink at her, and she seemed grateful.

She held her hands out in front of her face. They were rich with red soil, drying and forming cracks.

"We're going to look like crazy people when we leave here," she said.

"Let's not leave," I said.

She rested a hand on my leg, squeezed. I heard her laugh.

"What?"

Her voice was soft, almost sleepy. "Wouldn't that be fun."

I turned my head, looked at her profile. "I kind of need to stay a couple more days," I said. Licked my lips. "I think I might have to fill in for the last show. The girl who was supposed to do it had an emergency." I tried not to think of Stephanie, in her rusting Honda, hauling north to help Steven, the other pea in her pod.

Mom's face tilted toward me, calm again, the artful angles back in their right place. "The last show? Do they still do the Mermaid Queen?"

"Yeah," I said. "I think I'm the only one here who knows the routine."

I heard her breathe out fast, proud for me, in spite of everything.

We got up and held hands as we walked over slippery clay to the ladder. Mom went up first, then I followed. I brought the flashlight up and hooked it onto the top rung so Dylan could find it again the next time he came back. Then I stepped out into the cool night above.

The tank gave off light from within, like a jewel.

In the glow, I could see my body smeared with the reddish mud from the cave below. Spots had even started to dry and crack. My skin could have belonged to someone else, someone old. Someone who had seen years of harsh weather and carried the scars to prove it.

I looked over at Mom. She was covered in the same drying clay. For once, we looked alike, like mother and daughter.

"Do we tell Mel about all this?" I asked her.

Mom was looking at her legs, her arms, her hands—every part of her was covered in mud. She suddenly seemed very tired.

"Or Dad?" I added, my eyes widening as I realized how much this changed everything for everyone. "Should we tell him?"

Mom lifted her hands to rub her face, then thought again. She rolled her head on her neck—I could hear bones cracking, releasing tension.

She finally shrugged. "I don't know."

"But we have to figure this stuff out," I said.

"One thing at a time, Amy," she said. "I need to think all this through. You probably do too. I never expected you to know all this. Please. Let's just go."

I was going to fight it, but then I saw her face, the tired eyes. She looked like she was struggling to keep it together. "Okay," I said. I reached down and closed the double doors in the hillside. "That's probably a good idea."

Mom slid her hand to my shoulder and held me like that as we walked back to the station wagon.

CHAPTER *Seventeen*

FOR THE NEXT TWO NIGHTS, I BARELY SLEPT AT ALL.

It was all jumbled together inside me, the hugeness of what I'd learned—lies from my mother, truths about the father who'd made me and the one who'd raised me. And swirled up with all of it, images of my mother the Mermaid Queen and a mixture of excitement and fear like nothing I'd ever felt about performing the part myself. Mom had driven the station wagon back to Philly for Tom to use, then taken the bus back to the beach, where Mel, Lynne, and I met her at the bus station. She wrapped me and Mel in a sleepy hug and said, "I missed you guys." Neither of us had asked about Tom and what he'd said when he found out Mom was coming back here without him.

Back at the motel, Mel and I stayed up late, eating a tube of raw chocolate chip cookie dough we found in the back of Lynne's fridge.

After three quiet spoonfuls, Mel said, "I bet he was mad."

I nodded, peeled back the wrapper a little more. Without sarcasm, I said, "What else is new?"

"I'm afraid to go back."

I turned toward her, Indian style on the sofa bed. "I wonder what he thinks now, knowing we're all down here. All together in one place he's got Lynne, who's never batted an eye at all his bullying . . . Mom, who he's got this insane fifth-grade crush on . . . me, the one who loses it five times a day and screams at him to go to hell—"

"You *do* scream a lot," Mel said, reaching for another spoonful.

I made a face. "Then there's you, the one who can charm him so much that he forgets he's supposed to be a mean jerk. . . ."

"*I* do that?"

"What?"

She rolled her eyes. "Charm him?"

"Mel, of course. In a good way, though. I wish I could do that. I can't. That's why I scream so much."

"I screamed a lot this summer," she said quietly. "You know, not at first, but after a while, when he was just constantly *on* me all the time. No matter what I did, he was crouched in a doorway somewhere, waiting to jump out of the shadows and scream at me about it."

"Yeah." I nodded. "But you could always handle him before."

She shrugged. "I think without you there telling him to go to hell every couple of days, he gets a little . . . bolder. More aggressive."

I could see that.

She said, "Who knew all your yelling was actually like an important public service in our house."

"Well, luckily there will be two of us again to scream daily go-to-hells."

"Three, if you count Mom," she said. "Yuck—hide this," handing me her spoon.

"You know, he's probably scared to death, thinking we're all down here talking sense into Mom," I said, putting her spoon on the coffee table.

She scooted down to lie flat and pulled the sheet up to her chin. Her small fingers bent over the top of the sheet. She yawned and said, "There's no talking sense when it comes to Mom and men."

I looked at her, surprised. When had she come up with that?

She took the remote and clicked through till she found the Cartoon Network.

After a while, when I thought she was asleep, I heard her say softly into her pillow, "Thanks for not giving me crap about the book."

I touched her elbow gently with my own so she'd know I'd heard. Twirled a strand of her long hair around my finger, like she used to do to me when she was little, and just kept twirling it, soft like that, till she fell asleep.

But I still couldn't sleep.

Through two consecutive *What's New, Scooby-Doo?*s and an

infomercial starring fitness celebrity John Basedow, my tired eyes
wouldn't let go.

In the courtyard, I found Lynne's old rusting bike—one of
those big cruisers, meant for long flat rides down the boardwalk.
I'd never taken it to work because I didn't want to make her suspicious since I was only supposed to be going a few blocks. That
night, I started playing with it just for something to do. It actually
rode better than I thought it would, so I took it out to the street—
dark and quiet at 2 a.m., just riding up and down. The wind lifted
my hair. Crossing distance so fast like this, it felt good.

So I kept going.

I rode up the boardwalk, out past the park, and kept going up
the highway, avoiding looking at the dark ditches by the roadside—but still my mind couldn't help thinking, *That ditch there, is
that where Skip died? Or was it here, at this curve in the road?* I
thought I was lost in the cornfields until I saw it, the little brick
house and the foot of the giant steel tower. Little white and red
lights winked at the end of each branch, in no order, in no
rhythm. I stood at the foot of Bruce's driveway, catching my
breath, still trying to make sense of it.

On the patio beside the house, I saw movement in the hammock. A sleepy voice, Bruce's, said, "Who's there?"

Damn. My tires in the gravel—the noise had woken him. I
wondered quickly, should I just ride off? Then I had the clear
thought, if he wanted to badly enough, he could catch me, and
that would be more embarrassing.

So I said, "It's just me, Amy. From the park."

"I know you're from the park," he said. His head rose above the edge of the hammock. If he thought it was strange that I was there at this hour, I couldn't tell. Maybe he was used to late visitors. "Come where I can see you."

I walked up to the patio. Suddenly tired. Leaned the bike against the house, sat on the picnic bench, the dew cool on the backs of my thighs. Tried to come up with anything I could think about, other than him and the weirdness of being there at his house. And what that meant to me and should have meant to him. I wasn't ready to tell him who I was—didn't know if I'd *ever* be ready. Dumping it on him without planning it out would be bad. A blow like that was too hard to take. I knew that firsthand.

So I said, "Summer's almost over," just for something to say.

"Mm-hmm, another summer," he said, his voice thick from the angle he was lying at. The hammock swayed a little, and I wondered suddenly if he had fallen back asleep.

Tall corn around us stretched on and on. The tower watched over it all. He must've seen me looking up at it.

"Craziest thing one night," he said.

"What? The tower?"

"Birds love that thing," he said. "Sit on it all the time squawking away. Pisses off the phone company."

I laughed.

"They put up this speaker—supposed to put out a sound humans can't hear but birds hate. To keep 'em away," he said. "So one night I'm out here—I have a hard time sleeping, I come out here and pass the time—so I'm out here, and the speaker kicks on, and all the birds start flying around like crazy. Into each other. Into the tower. Straight down into the ground at full speed. Can you imagine that? Diving headfirst into the ground like that?"

"God," I said, horrified.

"Next day, I go back there. Find a bunch of dead birds, some of 'em actually impaled right on cornstalks. The most horrible thing I've ever seen." Cleared his throat, a wet sound. "So I call the phone company and they think I'm nuts. I come out here the next night to see it again and nothing."

"Well, what was it?"

"Don't know," he said. "Never happened again."

Those poor birds, confused, all they needed to do was follow their eyes instead of their ears.

"I see you're still coming out here at night, though."

"Still can't sleep," he said with a yawn.

"Yeah," I said. "Me neither."

Stephanie called the next morning. "Hey, Aim, it's me," she said, her voice sounding strained and very far away.

"God, are you okay? Is Steven okay?"

"Everyone's okay. Even Steven's poor ninety-five-pound *ex*-room-mate, who he decided to punch in the nose, is going to be fine."

"What happened?"

"He thought the guy was trying to break into his room. At least that's what he says. They'd been living together for two weeks, but from what I can tell, I think Steven forgot he had a new roommate."

"So, what—will they give him his own room now?"

"Well, not exactly. This has happened before. So they're giving him the boot."

"Can they just do that?" I was surprised by the anger in my voice.

She sighed. "I can't blame them, actually," she said. "They gave him two more chances than they had to. So now we're moving him to a new place, a nice one. I'm going to stay a few weeks to help him get used to it."

"Emma said you might push school back to the spring," I said.

"If I have to, yeah."

As I slid onto one of the kitchen bar stools, I shook my head, amazed at how easy it was for her to sacrifice . . . anything, really, for her brother. At the table, Mel poured herself a bowl of cereal, and I grabbed her a spoon from the drawer, thinking how hard the summer had been for her, alone like that. Mel took the spoon and mouthed, "Thank you." Things were going to be much different when we got home.

"So how's practice going?" she asked. "You've got the routine, right?"

"Yeah," I said, trying to sound light. She had enough to worry about. "I mean, I'm no *you*, but I think I'll do okay."

In reality, the fin took some getting used to.

Without Stephanie's help, it had been a long few days.

The other girls were okay. It was just Heather, still, who rubbed me wrong. Around the bend from the ticket counter that day, I'd heard her talking to Bruce.

"How come *she* gets to do it? Are you sure she even knows what she's doing?" I cringed, pressing myself flat against the mossy fence, hoping they didn't see me. She went on, unaware of me there. "Anyway, it should be my turn."

"Do you know it?" Bruce's rough voice was direct, loud.

My cheeks flushed, the kind of red that traveled all the way down my chest—he was going to give away my part.

He repeated, "Do you *know* the routine?"

Heather paused. "Most of it."

Bruce sighed heavily. "You don't know it. And you just hate it that Amy does. And that she's good at it."

His slow footsteps moved away, and I could picture him heading up to the control room, where he would watch over things.

When Lynne heard we were going to the beach, she found a third pink beach chair that matched the other two and shooed us away, saying we should go enjoy some mother-daughter bonding time. "It's your last day here," she said. "You should enjoy yourselves."

"You're just trying to get rid of us so you can root through my purse for candy," Mom teased.

"Who's the godmother and who's the godchild here?" Lynne said. She swatted Mom on her butt, hustling her toward the door.

Mom shuffled away playfully, covering her backside with her straw beach hat.

We set up our chairs at the waterline, one two three, with Mom in the middle.

"I wish we had a pool," Mom said, digging her heels into the wet sand. "Back home, I mean."

The mention of "back home" had quieted Mel. I shielded my eyes from the sun, looking out to the horizon, where boats sailed on this smooth day.

I heard Mel say, "Maybe we could come down here again next summer."

"Maybe," Mom said casually. "But I don't think Tom was so crazy about it."

A deep breath escaped me too loudly. Mom rolled her head to my side, waiting.

"Well," I said calmly, meeting her gaze, "I love it here."

Mel leaned up so she could look past Mom at me. "I do too," she said.

Mom looked back and forth from Mel to me, our serious expressions telling her there was more to this conversation than vacation choices. Her gaze finally settled on me. Her look was questioning.

I touched her hand on the armrest of her chair. "You love it here too."

She pressed her lips together, squinting at me through one eye.

"All I'm saying is, that counts for something. Or at least I think it does." No sarcasm there. My voice didn't shake either, not one bit.

Mom looked back out to the ocean, the same gray-green as her eyes. Mel and I sat back and relaxed too, and every once in a while, way out in the water, we'd catch a glimpse of a dolphin or two, swimming south, toward warm water.

CHAPTER *Eighteen*

THE LAST SHOW OF THE SEASON, BRUCE AND EMMA WOULD GIVE FREE tickets to some of the locals, and most of the girls' parents came. Mom and Lynne were there with Mel. Tom was driving down to get us that night, already on his way.

Earlier, I'd climbed up to the deck to peek out. It was more crowded than usual in the bleachers, and the girls buzzed about it when they came through the tube from their third song.

"Whoo-hoo!" Ally, happy, lifted herself out of the tube and lay back on the floor. Her heavy makeup looked strange in the fluorescent light of the shack.

"Nice speed on that return." Carrie scooted up, leaving room for Maria and Heather to slip in and go through the tunnel for the fourth song. She was breathing hard, already unzipping her fin.

The one I got to wear was a little special—Emma had pulled it out of the shed and handed it to me that night. Rather than being shiny, heavy satin spandex flecked with sequins, the whole thing, the whole entire surface, was covered in sequins. Ten shades of blue and green, each the size of a dime and sewn on so they moved and dangled and danced in the light, looking alive underwater.

I pulled at the straps of my top to check that they were tight enough. On my head, I wore a green-gold headband. Into the back were tucked corners of a veil. Thin layers of gold, sea blue, silver, soft, sheer, flowing. It streamed behind me like tendrils of seaweed.

I ran my hand over my lap, watching each sequin. Little reflections of myself looked back at me, hundreds of them. My mom's mouth. My . . . dad's hair, these spirals, out of control, like his. And a dance that belonged to all of us.

Maria was first to arrive through the tunnel. I could see her face, bubbles streaming from her nose. She smiled big as she reached the surface. Heather next. They lifted themselves out and cleared the way for me.

"Go, Amy," Maria said with a smile. "Bring it on home."

I slid into the water, took one, two, three deep breaths, then under. I pulled myself along the tunnel by the handles and emerged among the kelp strands.

The sound of my heart was slow and stable. I paused, waiting for my music cue—the calypso arc, it was coming. Took a final breath from the lowest hose and pushed myself off the tank and into the light.

Glimpses. That's all I could catch. One moment, a reflection of myself, the sequins dancing as I arched back into three perfect O loops, my hands brushing the tip of the fin, reminding me, *Yes, this is really happening.*

Then a row of blurry faces, lots of them, in the bleachers as I snake-kicked around the tank, building up speed. The flash of a camera. Was that Mom's face I saw? I stopped for a breath here and there, and then I went into the final sequence.

I chased the trail of my veil as I did a series of figure-eight loops. Like a coin spinning on its edge, the loops got slower and slower. Finally at a stop, I raised my arms and tilted my face upward.

And as if pulled by a string, I rose to the top.

Broke the surface.

I swung myself up on the deck, unzipped the fin, and slipped it off so I could dangle my feet in the water for one last feel. In case I wouldn't be back, I wanted to remember it this way.

By the time we were done saying goodbyes, the bleachers were empty and I was going to be late meeting everyone back at the motel so we could get on the road.

I changed into a khaki skirt and a black spaghetti strap shirt made of the world's softest cotton.

My hair was wet—it would dry as I ran.

Down the roadside and up to the boardwalk, my legs were light and fast. One sandal in each hand because they slowed me down too much.

Up near Lynne's, the block before, I heard my name being called. "Amy! Amy!" I turned, still moving. Curt was waving. He held out a softball to me. "Free throw?" he called with a smile.

"Hey!" I said, waving over my shoulder. "Sorry—gotta run."

Turning, in the blackened windows of the video game arcade, I saw my reflection. The curve of my strong shoulders. Carefree stride, quickly carrying me where I needed to go, on bare feet. Long waves in my hair, streaming back as I faced the wind head-on.

Never once stopping to glance over my shoulder and wonder what I was leaving behind, what I should've done instead.

We were gathering in the motel office, and I ran out to get a snack for the road. I rocked the candy machine back on its wobbly legs to dislodge the sourdough pretzels I'd just bought, which had gotten stuck. Behind me, I heard the tentative flip-flop of shoes coming to a stop. "Here, I'll get that for you."

Dylan. Lynne had said she'd told him I was leaving. That he should stop by.

I stepped back to let him rock the machine for me, fixing my eyes on the floor. "They should have a sign on this that says, 'In case of an emergency, break glass.'"

He laughed. "So. You're leaving." A last bang and the pretzels dropped out, along with a pack of fruit chews.

I leaned my hand on the machine front and said, "I am."

We both stood there for a second. I stared at his flip-flops. The white moon at the base of each toenail.

"Hug?" he said.

I took ahold of his shoulders and leaned into him, feeling his strong arms around my waist. His warm palms rested on my back; they felt soothing. I squeezed harder, letting the sides of our faces touch, pressing our ears close. Cupped together for a second, in our ears I could hear the faraway sound of the ocean.

I pulled back and smiled as I said, "I think I swung coming back next summer."

He grinned, almost shyly. "How did you do that?"

"Bribery."

His smile broadened. Shifted his weight from one foot and back to the other.

Neither of us knew what to do, so I said it, what I'd been thinking: "Do over?"

A laugh this time. He said, "Do overs suck."

I tilted my head to one side. "Not always."

"You want to write me?" he said.

"Yeah, I do. Or call. Let's do that."

I ripped the lid off the fruit chews box and got my lip liner out of my pocket. "Here, my number." I wrote it down and handed it to him and then wrote his down on the other piece of the lid as he said it aloud, then folded it in half and tentatively kissed it as he watched, feeling a little silly.

Meeting his eyes, I saw he was touched.

"They're waiting for me, so I'd better—"

He nodded and we quickly hugged. I knew we would talk. Felt for the paper in my pocket, a lucky charm.

Then Tom's voice carried through the din of air conditioners chugging in the warm night—"Jee-sus Christ."

I felt the pull back to the office, where Mel and Mom were waiting to leave.

I entered the office on quiet feet. Hunched over the tiny black-and-white TV on the counter, Tom watched something, his face too close to the screen. Lynne and Mom, in the waiting room chairs, chatted quietly—then Lynne took my hand and said, "You were great."

"She was," Mom said to her. Then to me, "You were. Truly."

We both looked away, eyes wet. Earlier, we had decided that we would tell Mel and Tom, and then my dad, about Skip. But not here. That we would save for home.

Enough had happened in Wildwood already.

And I still had time to figure out the best way to tell Bruce. It didn't seem so urgent, like the others. But I wanted him to know.

Melissa sat on the floor, playing with Lynne's dog. She tossed its ball against the wall, watched it jump and miss, then tossed it again. On the next toss, the dog nearly got it, bounced it higher with his nose. It hit the TV antenna with a clatter. Static filled the room.

"Damn it!" Tom shouted.

Mel shrank back, cringing—I saw it. The dog yipped, wanting the ball.

Tom leaned over the counter, yelled down at Mel, "What the fuck was that?" She didn't even bother to look up.

I'd been down this road before. There was no good exit.

So I caught his eye, and once I had it, I said to him, "It was an accident. Sorry about that. My fault—I banged it."

I felt Mel look at me. She smiled.

Tom's face tilted up. We were eye to eye, with him on the stool like that. Right in my face, he cupped his hands around his mouth and in a mock-announcer voice he shouted, "Ladies and gentlemen! Please join me in welcoming back to the stage, after her three-month hiatus, Super-klutz." He started a loud round of applause alone.

Silence filled the room. He waited.

I didn't take the bait.

Finally, I said, "I apologized. You don't have to get mean." I held his eyes until he looked away, at Mom. Her glare was icy.

"The train is leaving!" he shouted. And while the announcer voice was there, it had been taken down a notch. I think we all noticed it.

It was midnight, Tom's preferred travel time.

I sat with my luggage in the way back—the rear-facing jump-seat whose name conjured images of pouncing or something predatory or adventurous, but in truth I was there only because it made Mel motion sick, and we both wanted to lie down.

Have you ever ridden looking out the back window of a station wagon?

The moon follows you. And it makes you sleepy.

Dreams grabbed at the corners of my eyes but still wouldn't come fully.

By 1 a.m., I thought I was the only passenger awake. Then I heard a piece of hushed conversation from the front seat.

"I saw a cop back there, hon. You might want to watch your speed," Mom said, low and quiet.

Tom's anger had been stewing. He'd been looking for an in. "This trip was a fucking waste of time," he said. "You should have just brought her back last week."

I sank lower in the seat, my shoulders pulling in. Wanting to practice being as invisible as possible.

Then clearer, louder from the front seat, I heard my mom say, "No, Tom, I know what my daughters need."

Goose bumps raised the hairs on my arms.

After a while, we were on I-95 near home, just past the Walt Whitman Bridge, and from the clacking pistons and revved engine I knew that Tom's foot had the gas pushed to the floor. He was overtaking the few sleepy cars on the road with fury, cutting them too close, giving the wagon its moment of full, pure glory.

My tongue was thick and my lids were heavy; I craved sleep like a drug.

Before my eyes closed, I recognized the familiar landscape of our exit, which Tom would too late realize we had zoomed past. This would piss him off, I knew—I could always so clearly see Tom's imperfections.

But now, I could tell, they would haunt me less. Tom would never be perfect. None of us ever would be, really.

I was rocked over the edge into deep sleep, calmed and thrilled by this knowledge.

Acknowledgments

Special thanks to Luanne Smith, a truly inspiring teacher.

To my editor, Liesa Abrams, thanks for your talent, dedication, and friendship, and to Eloise Flood and Kristen Pettit for your gracious support.

Finally, many thanks to Colleen Rush and also to Maria Neuman and Pat Tobin. This book would not exist without you.

Visit bethmayall.com.